THE MERMAN'S KISS

A STEAMY MYTHOLOGY ROMANCE

TAMSIN LEY

A Production of

Twin Leaf
Press

BRIANNA DROPPED THE pregnancy test into the bathroom trash and joined Eric in bed. He had his laptop across his knees, studying one of his corporate financial projection reports.

"Negative," she said, fighting the crack in her voice. The sheets felt frigid against her skin.

Without looking away from the screen, he reached over and patted her shoulder. "We'll try again next month."

After a stillborn baby girl almost two years ago, they'd followed the doctor's advice to wait a year before trying again. Now another year had passed without a ray of hope. What if she'd lost her only chance to be a mother?

A tear leaked from the corner of her eye, soaking into the pillow. "Maybe we should stop trying."

"If that's what you want." He scrolled the mouse.

Brianna's chest ached. "Eric?"

"Mmm?" He tapped his finger against the mouse pad.

"Eric." Her voice did crack this time. At least he looked away from the computer. His eyes reminded her of the fish in the tank at his office, round and dark and emotionless. She swallowed her tears and slid her head forward to rest her cheek on his arm. "Make love to me."

His forearm bunched as he pulled it from beneath her. Her chest lightened for a single heartbeat, then his arm settled back down around the top of her pillow. He patted between her shoulder blades and returned his gaze to the computer. "It's late. We'll try again next cycle."

THE SALTY BREEZE blowing across the pier tasted of tears. Behind her, a few scattered people went about their off-season business along the boardwalk. Ahead, only empty, colorless gray sky and water.

Brianna stepped off the pier.

The heavy fishing weights cinched around her waist did their job, pulling her toward the bottom quickly enough to make her ears pop.

She'd heard drowning wasn't a bad way to go, but the salty water stung her eyes and nose. And the water was cold. Really cold. As the light above faded to a murky blue, she watched the final pockets of air billow upward from her blouse. Who knew the bottom was this far down? A school of fish blocked the meager light a moment, and then they were gone.

Her chest burned with need, but she was afraid to take a breath. Was she sure she wanted to do this? She and Eric had been married three years before she'd realized he was such a cold fish and would never change. Even the stillbirth of little Pauline hadn't seemed to touch him. But he also wasn't the only fish in the sea. Would divorce be so bad? Just before he'd died, her father had made her swear never to divorce her husband. Her mother's abandonment had torn out a part of his soul. So she'd promised.

But he was gone now. This was her life.

Or her death.

This is stupid! She snatched at the rope belt weighing heavy against her hips. The entire thing was full of knots where she'd attached the five-pound weights. Which knot was holding it closed? Her loose blouse, useful to hide the weights on land, billowed in the current. She couldn't see the knots. With both hands, she lifted her shirt hem and pulled the garment over her head. The water's greedy clutches swept it away.

Her bottom bounced against the seafloor, sending up a cloud of silt. A surge of bubbles forced themselves from between her lips. She clamped her mouth shut. The air escaped from her nose instead. Her tortured lungs burned like they might explode.

Her left foot scraped stone, and she tried to stand. To push toward the surface. The rock slid out from under her as the tide carried her out to sea.

She was so stupid. Why had she thought she wanted to die? And like this, as fish food? Eyes burning in the salt water and straining in the light, she searched for the right knot. Her fingers were numb with cold. Tingly. More air trickled from her nose. Her lungs cried out for her to take a breath.

The light grew dimmer. With both hands, she pushed at the belt, trying to squeeze it down around her hips. The rope stretched a little. Maybe she could shimmy out of it. Except the waistband of her capri pants thwarted that idea. She flicked open the button and slid them down her legs, taking her panties with them. Kicking, she released the fabric to the tide.

Without her consent, her lungs sipped a draught of water, and she doubled over with a cough. Then her lungs were full. There was no air to cough. Her naked legs scraped along the rocky bottom.

Her vision was going dark from lack of oxygen. Or was the water getting deeper? A strange calm settled over her. Another school of fish blocked the murky light. She blinked. Maybe death wouldn't be so bad. Like falling asleep. And maybe her baby would be waiting for her on the other side.

Strong hands grabbed her arms above the elbows. A man with spiky hair and glinting eyes stared into her face. Someone had come to save her! She flung her arms about his neck. Or at least she tried. The water slowed her motion. Both her legs wrapped around his waist like she might climb him to the surface.

His eyes widened, metallic silver beneath a dark brow line. Smooth skin slid beneath her fingertips. His face drew closer, eyes boring into hers. A firm mouth found hers, and his tongue slid in.

She gasped, the lightheadedness of drowning turning into the twirling water-ballet of desire. Like a lure, the dancing tongue within her called on instincts she didn't know she possessed. Created a pulsing throb in her core, a need greater than air. She bent her head and matched the kiss, tangling her tongue with his and sending rockets of electricity straight to her core. Her entwined legs drew her hips against his. Ground against the hard line of an erection.

A drawn-out note—not quite a groan, not quite a song— surrounded her. Penetrated deep into her bones. He drew back, hands on her hips. The kiss continued in a teasing mockery of consummation.

For a split second, she wondered if this was the result of a final, dying fantasy. An attempt of her mind to protect her from the horror of death. But then the moment was gone, and all she knew was need. Need to be one with him. To feel him inside her. To cast away death with the very act that created life.

Legs still locked around him, she pulled him close again. Arched to meet him. Silently pleaded for more.

And as naturally as breathing, his cock filled her.

What...? The thought echoed in her brain, as if she were hearing his thoughts as well as her own.

Yet she had no time to pause and consider. His hands slithered down to cup her ass, drawing her closer. He undulated against her like a wave.

Dizzy with ecstasy, she bucked her hips in time to his rhythm. Threw her head back so the angle of their joining stroked her innermost ridges. Shivers rocketed down her thighs, pooled in the core of her belly. This was primal. A need greater than she'd known could exist. A demand blocking out all thoughts of anything but satisfaction.

All around them, the current swirled as he thrust. Pure instinct made her clamp her legs tighter about his waist. Nothing mattered now but the climax. The heady release of something larger than she'd ever experienced before. Heat flushed her, searing her from head to toe. Tumbling thoughts collided with each other inside her head. Sex. *Magic.* Heat. *Breath.* Life. *Yes!*

She screamed the last word, throwing her head back as her orgasm shook her.

The man's fingers dug deep into her buttocks as he joined her.

Eyes closed, chest heaving from exertion, she relaxed in his arms. Her heartbeat pulsed in her ears, and her limbs felt limp as jellyfish. Sex had always been bland with Eric. Clinical. She'd sought to please him but never found the ecstasy so many of her friends carried on about. Now she knew what the fuss was.

A muscular arm fastened about her waist, and a surge of water pushed her hair off her face. She opened her eyes, her breath catching in her throat. Then she stiffened. Breath? She was breathing. How was she breathing?

The weights she wore dug into her hip as he held her close against him. With amazing force, he propelled them through the water, focused on something ahead. Her gaze raked his spiked hair and naked shoulder. Down his back, his spine rose into a pronged fan. *A fin?*

She blinked, wondering if her eyes were playing tricks on her in the murky light. She was underwater. But breathing. She slid a hand across his shoulder blade and up the fin to the first bony prong. Craning her head, she looked down the length of his body. Salt water rose in her throat. Where legs should be, a silver tail ended in a billowing fin. *This guy has a tail.*

She'd just had sex with a merman. And now he was carrying her deeper into the sea.

CHAPTER 2

*T*HE FEMALE'S WARMTH coursed through his bloodstream like a drug. Zantu had seen her struggling and had meant only to check her body for salvage, a weakness of his inherited from his father. The glint of gold around her throat had made him dare to approach. Then she'd wrapped herself around him like a squid. A very hot squid. His cock had erupted from its sheath like a narwhal's horn through ice, ready to claim her heat before his brain even had time to process the act. The irrevocable act.

And now the green-eyed beauty owned him, body and soul.

Unlike the more promiscuous mer-females who would search out and copulate with anything with a penis, mermen bonded for life. A merman who bonded was doomed to a life of misery as his mate strayed again and again. He would raise the children, coddling them like a father sea horse until they, too, left him. Most mermen died of broken hearts.

Zantu gritted his teeth and tightened his grip around his new mate. He'd felt her stiffen, likely to flee into the arms of another man now that she'd taken what she wanted. But Zantu wasn't about to let that happen. He was determined to find a way to bond her to him as tightly as he was bonded to her.

He would find a way to harness this capricious female heart.

The woman struggled in his grip, flailing uselessly as he dove over the first chasm toward the nesting grounds. Her nails dug into the flesh on his shoulder, and her naked legs slid along his tail.

Legs.

He'd never imagined bonding to a human. Mermaids seduced men all the time, but mermen, lacking a female's seductive skills, avoided contact at all costs. Many a tale warned of humans hunting mermen for sport.

As the woman struggled, the bush covering her female parts brushed his hip, hot and inviting. His cock stirred again at the invitation. He'd been told the bond would be strong when it happened, but the draw he felt was as inevitable as the tide. He adjusted his grip so she was beneath him, looking up, her eyes fixed on him. She opened her mouth as if to speak, but no sound emerged. Was she mute? Perhaps she was out of oxygen? The magic in his kiss should have enabled her to breathe as easily as a deep-sea dweller until the moon went dark. Then the magic would have to be renewed, or she would drown. At least that was what the mermaids said about the men they seduced. But perhaps a merman's kiss wasn't as strong?

After glancing forward to be sure he was on course, he dipped his head toward her and covered her mouth with his. Her lips were incredibly soft, working against his as she continued to try to speak. Her hands crept over his shoulders and slid along his dorsal, sending shivers across his skin. Desire rose in him again, and he crushed her tighter against him, all thoughts of forward momentum banished as he plunged his tongue between her blunt teeth, twirled, and thrust. His shaft once again unsheathed itself, ready for another bonding.

Her legs fluttered, and he curled his tail up and between them, pressing his hips to hers. Her heat was waiting, slick and hot. Her legs around him tightened like a trap, and her soft breasts burned against his chest. Her mouth tasted like sunlight-dappled waves.

What am I doing? The thought wasn't his. Depths, he was truly done for. Only the strongest of bonds allowed a merman to hear his mate's thoughts. The only bond more rare was when the female could hear the male.

He opened his eyes. Maybe... Her lids were closed, her lips swollen with kisses. *Stay with me,* he thought. She threw back her head, mouth forming soundless words, but her hands kept tight hold against his shoulders. Maybe she heard him. Maybe not. All he could do was hold her as close as he could as long as he could.

Crushing her against him, he trailed kisses down her throat. One hand found her breast and cupped it, teasing the nipple into a coral nub. She shuddered, and her nails dug into his back as her depths tightened around him. His testicles throbbed for release, but he refused to let the moment be over so soon. He drew back until the tip of his member just teased her folds. In his mind, he heard her whimper, plead for more.

Not yet. I'm not done with you.

She wriggled her hips against him, pressing her clit along his waiting length. Her tongue roved her lips, inviting him to taste, but he resisted, simply gazing upon her, fighting his own desire. To exercise such control was as heady as mounting her. The drive was strong in him, but not overpowering. How was he doing this? A merman was supposed to be unable to resist his mate's lust, even for a moment, as doomed to her whims as a jellyfish to the tide. If he could hold off like this, perhaps there was hope for him.

Then she opened her eyes, and her lips mouthed, "Please." He was indeed doomed. With a shudder he sheathed himself inside her, slammed his hips against her. She matched his rhythm, throwing her head back and rocking with him until his tail curled in the ecstasy of release.

He sagged against her, holding her gently and allowing the current to carry them where it would. For thirty-five years he'd avoided his bond-fate, sidestepping many tempting offers in the process. Of late, his biology had nearly toppled him into the abyss on several occasions. A raven-haired seductress with a voice like an orca's. A green-tailed enchantress with a golden dorsal fin he later learned had been tipped with love toxin.

And yet, now that he was bonded, he was relieved. No longer would he need to live in terror of other mermaids. Of traps and subterfuge. And perhaps with a human, he would be able to maintain some control. Maybe even shrug off the curse of his bond-fate.

A war raged inside his chest as he held his mate close while some distant, protected part of his mind plotted a way to be free of her.

But for now, he'd do everything in his power to protect her.

CHAPTER 3

*B*RIANNA FLOATED BONELESS as sea kelp, luxuriating in the afterglow of the merman's lovemaking. As primal as the act had been, she still thought of it as lovemaking. She could have sworn he'd whispered his devotion in her ear as they'd coupled. Or perhaps it was just her subconscious desire to be loved and cherished.

She opened heavy lids but could see nothing beyond the shoulders of the merman in the inky depths. Featureless. Maybe this was all a dream and she was dead. Could you dream when you were dead? Whatever the case, she never wanted to wake up. Not if death was like this. With a sigh, she wrapped her arms around the merman's waist and pressed her cheek against his shoulder. He smelled briny and herbal at the same time.

I wonder what his name is.

A voice like a song came to her. *Zantu.*

She giggled, bubbles tickling her nose. *Now I'm hearing voices. What kind of a name is Zantu?*

The palm he'd been stroking against the small of her back stopped. He thrust her away to look into her face, his hands like claws around her biceps. *You can hear me?*

His silver eyes flashed fiercely, and he grinned; every one of his pearly whites was sharp as a canine. How had she not noticed that while they'd kissed? For the first time, she was afraid.

Can you hear me? The sonorous voice again floated through her mind.

A shiver started in her chest and rattled outward through her bones. Her heart raced until her vision jostled with every pounding beat. She managed to nod at him.

He released one hand from her bicep and stroked her cheek.

She recoiled at the sight of the slight webbing between his fingers. A word formed in her mind as his gyrating tail caught her attention. *Monster.*

His hand hovered millimeters from her cheek, and she swung her gaze up to meet his, suddenly horrified that he'd heard. His mouth no longer smiled. His liquid-silver eyes gleamed like twin moons. *I'm sorry,* she thought, hoping he could hear her.

He sucked in his cheeks as if willing himself not to speak and dropped the hand from her face. *Come.*

His other hand slid down her arm to take her hand, and he turned away. With a powerful thrash of his tail, he pulled her along behind him, towing her like a bit of flotsam.

ZANTU'S JOY about the discovery of the reciprocal, telepathic bond tasted like seagull spatter on his tongue. She thought him an abomination? A monster? Of course she did. Her kind hunted his. There could be no love between them.

I'm Brianna, she thought to him, but he didn't answer. He couldn't. He had to find a way to break this unholy bond before he revealed all the secrets of the mer-kingdom to an outsider. Before she could rally her people to hunt them down in their nests.

Pumping his tail muscles like he was fleeing an orca's teeth, he plunged them through the tidal current toward the deeper water where he could hold her until he'd formed a plan. The swim would normally take him less than a quarter tide, but with his mate's extra weight, he couldn't move nearly as fast. He surveyed the waters ahead, wary of sharks and other predators who might take advantage of his handicap.

A trill of laughter caught his attention, followed by three scale notes and the underlying vibrations of a fish-harp. His dorsal fin flattened against his back. Mermaids. Melody lilted through the water, a familiar cadence, a magic to incite desire. He knew that voice. Loia. She'd tempted him before, nearly caught him in her net. But now he felt only the faintest acknowledgement of her song's power. His bond was set, and she could no longer influence him.

Fin flaring tall and straight, he readjusted his course to carry him directly toward the music. He couldn't wait to see her face when she realized she'd lost him.

In the center of a shoal of tiny, silver fish, he spotted the curvaceous indigo tail fin of the songstress. The fish darted and flashed in time to her voice, falling and rising and spinning around in a magical haze. Her hair billowed outward like a blueberry sea fan, while her breasts, pale as alabaster and tipped with violet-blue nipples, bobbed like lures. Luscious indigo lips sang promises of bliss.

His throat tightened. Her magic was strong. Even with his ties to his new mate, the mermaid's song pulled at him, burned through his blood, and made his sheath swell as his cock surged in time with the dancing fish.

She spotted him. Her golden eyes narrowed and her lips curved into a predatory grin even as she continued her song. Her fingers caressed the tines of a fish-harp cradled in one arm, pulling notes from deep within each gold-tipped tine while she crooned of love and desire.

His mate's hand tightened around his fingers; for the barest moment he'd forgotten she was there. His heart thudded against his rib cage. He would be safe from the song because of his bond-mate. He pulled her up beside him and hooked an arm around her waist, delighting in the flicker of jealousy that crossed Loia's face.

"Zantu, what have you brought me?" she sang. "A pretty little feast?"

He held his woman tighter. "I've found my bond-mate. You have no more power over me, Loia."

The net of fish encircling the mermaid lost cohesion for a moment then re-formed, hovering like a million tiny blades ready to strike. "You cannot bond with a human. Their lives are over with a flick of the fin."

"Only because you abandon them to drown, Loia, lovesick and broken."

The mermaid undulated her tail and thrust forth her breasts suggestively. "Why would you even want her? She cannot play hide-and-seek with you among the kelp beds. Or race you along the canyon deeps. Or sing while you orgasm to your very bones. She can't even escape when a shark attacks. A human is no fit mate for our kind. They're barely useful as toys."

"You don't know that," he snapped. A tiny fish brushed his arm, and he shrugged it away. "Mermaids don't take mates." But her comments had him worried. How *would* he protect a human mate when predators invaded?

"We take plenty of mates, Zantu." Her grin exposed every one of her needle-sharp teeth, as if ready to devour him. "We just don't limit ourselves to one. A pity you will never experience a true lover's passion, only the clumsy limbs of a land-walker. Or... maybe she would like to play, too?" Loia spun in place, whipping her head around to find him again as she completed her turn. Her genital slit had pulsed open during her spin, exposing the pink invitation of her vulva. "Human men like to watch each other copulate. I could show her—and you— what a real female can do with a man."

Something caressed the opening of his sheath, and he looked down to find two tiny fish rubbing themselves against him. He looked back up and realized the rest of the school had engulfed them like a net.

Loia licked her lips and ran her hands up over her breasts to tweak her indigo nipples, arching her back. One hand traced lightly down her center line to massage the swollen folds of her labia. Her scent floated to him in the wake of her net of minions.

In spite of his bond to Brianna, Loia's overt sexuality was getting to him. The teasing at his groin had nearly burst his cock from its protective sheath. His head spun, and all he could think about was letting his urges free.

Brianna batted at a fish near her face and pressed herself closer to him, turning her face into his shoulder. *I want to go home.*

Those words sobered him faster than the strike of a moray eel. She wanted to leave him. He wrapped both arms around her and began to back away from Loia's seductions. If he wanted to keep his mate, staying near Loia wasn't the way to do it. "Go find some other man to ruin," he called out.

Loia's pale skin went lurid. Her lips spread thin as she bared every one of her shark-like teeth. "You cannot keep her," she shrilled.

Brianna wriggled in his grasp, her legs slapping his fin as if she wished to swim away. Her slender shoulders felt fragile in his grip, but he refused to let her go. The scent of blood reached his nose. Inside his head, he heard Brianna scream, *My legs!*

He loosed his hold and saw her lower extremities surrounded by Loia's net of fish. A trail of pink-clouded water floated in their wake. They were biting her. The blood would surely draw every predator within a league of them. Rage rose up inside him, and he opened his mouth wide to emit a deep, repelling sphere of sound.

The fish scattered.

CHAPTER 4

*T*HE SUDDEN BARITONE note Zantu emitted, so different from the tenor opera he'd been singing to the mermaid, vibrated deep into Brianna's bones. He pumped his tail, and a sudden surge of water forced her to close her eyes as they left the singing mermaid and her biting pets far behind.

Brianna's skin itched and burned where the tiny fish had nibbled her with razor-sharp teeth, but he was moving too fast for her to check her wounds. She buried her face against his warm neck and hung on for dear life. The mermaid's mesmerizing performance had grown more bizarre with every note that passed the female's lips. The final lewd sexual display left no doubt in Brianna's mind about what the creature wanted. And the pesky, biting fish made it very clear she'd prefer Brianna out of the picture.

She'd been frightened by the merman's differences only a short time earlier; now what frightened her about him also made her believe he could protect her. She rubbed her thighs together in memory of him between them. Why did he want her, when he was pursued by a creature as alluring as that mermaid? Even Brianna had felt that pull, and she'd never been attracted to another female in her life. No wonder sailors were said to willingly plunge to their deaths in pursuit of the creatures.

Looking back over her shoulder, she sought the mermaid in the gloomy water, sure the fierce female would pursue, but her eyes were too weak to pierce the midnight depths. The world had lost its color and become murky shades of black and green. A school of small fish slithered past, spear-shaped sides seeming to turn as one. Ahead, filaments rose from the seafloor to create a shifting curtain patterned by other sea creatures darting to and fro among them.

Zantu readjusted his grip around her waist, the pressure of his muscular arms making her skin quiver. She could feel his heartbeat beneath her fingers as he carried her ever deeper into the water. The way his tail bumped her legs and pubic bone as he swam reminded her of their earlier coupling. Made her yearn for more. But he showed no intention of slowing for another dalliance.

Colorful sea stars and anemones passed by in a rainbow blur in the rocks below. He continued to shoot through the forest, past a big red-and-black fish with a gaping mouth, over an eel peeking from the rocks. The forest here seemed thinner, with more light reaching the seafloor. Or maybe they were in shallower water? She looked upward at the canopy of fronds swaying in the current but couldn't judge how far away they were.

Where are you taking me?

Where you'll be safe.

His words eased the tension in her chest. Until that moment, she'd harbored a fear that with his lust satiated he might develop another hunger. One that used his razor-like teeth.

He slowed and pushed her away to look at her. *I'm not a monster.*

Guilt flushed her from head to toe. This whole "hearing each other's thoughts" thing was weirding her out. *I'm... sorry. I just don't know anything about you or your kind.*

We stay away from humans. You're dangerous.

A chuckle of bubbles left her mouth as she thought of that. Here she was, who knew how many feet below the sea, held captive by a sharp-toothed, web-fingered, sleek-tailed merman, and he claimed to be afraid of her. Yet when she met his silver-eyed gaze, she realized he was completely serious.

Zantu clutched his new mate to his side and torpedoed toward the kelp beds where he and the other mermen maintained the nesting grounds. Brianna's unfiltered thoughts reached him in irregular and unpredictable waves, one minute with disconcerting openness, the next not at all. He had no idea why. Most clear was her fear. Her curiosity. Her sensual attention to his skin against hers. The connection was driving him mad yet reassuring him at the same time. Although she thought him a monster, she wanted him as badly as he wanted her—at least for now. Would her interest wane like the females of his kind?

Ahead, the kelp swayed rhythmically between glistening shafts of filtered sunlight. Zantu dragged her into the foliage without halting, sending sonic commands to the plants and the creatures among it to clear the way. Those unfamiliar with the forest would be quickly lost and confused among the stalks, but he knew the path as well as he did his own tail. Strands of kelp caressed his skin with familiarity, loosing bubbles in his wake. Brianna clutched his neck tight enough for him to feel her racing heartbeat.

The kelp opened up to reveal his small refuge beneath the sea. Like the others of his sex, he'd created a haven fit for a queen, in spite of his determination to remain free of a bond-mate. Nesting was a biological imperative for his kind, mate or no mate.

His home had a floor of round, multicolored stones and wave-polished shells and glass. Items he'd salvaged from shipwrecks and lovingly restored filled the shallow depression: a rosewood table with three matching chairs, a vanity with a tall mirror still clear enough to see a reflection, a rocking chair inlaid with mother-of-pearl. A human bed with a fancy carved headboard rested in an alcove, mattress replaced by a soft garden of sponges. At the foot, an ancient ironbound chest held more treasures from his years of salvage. Around the clearing's edges, he'd cultivated a garden of fine, edible seaweed, decorative sea fans, and rock outcroppings covered with clusters of indigo and green mussels.

But his finest creation rested in the center of the nest, awaiting the day Zantu truly lost his freedom. Supported by living fingers of coral, a bassinet rocked evenly in the gentle ocean current.

In his mind, Brianna's thoughts swam with perceptions too jumbled for him to decipher. Or perhaps she was learning to guard her thoughts. There would eventually need to be a filter, if nothing else than to spare the other of the distraction of receiving every detailed impression.

He deposited her in the rocking chair, the fishing weights around her waist keeping her solidly planted against its seat, and pumped his tail once to back away from her. Spinning in a cautious circle, he surveyed the wall of kelp surrounding them. Loia's minions should have been blocked by the kelp forest, but he could take no chances they—and thereby she—might follow him to his refuge.

Satisfied they were alone, he faced his new mate, looking her over with what he hoped was an unbiased eye. Her hair, much shorter than any mermaid's and not nearly as colorful, floated in a dark halo about her face, and her speckled green eyes reminded him of sunlight through kelp fronds. Sun-kissed arms and legs transitioned to paler skin over her breasts and torso. Her deep-coral-peaked nipples bobbed lusciously above her smoothly muscled belly, and the tuft of hair between her legs made his cock stir as his eyes drifted over her hips and down her legs to her tiny painted toes.

A human.

He'd bonded with a human.

Had such a thing ever happened in the history of mer-kind? Certainly mermaids seduced human men, but never bonded. Not with mermen and certainly not with humans. The reclusive, emotionally susceptible mermen stayed far away from females of any kind—at least until a mermaid caught him. Just Zantu's luck to be seduced by a human. What was she doing in the ocean, anyway?

His gaze returned to the coarsely knotted belt around her hips. The weights he recognized as those used by fishermen seeking trophies. Such men were never gentle, and he'd helped many swordfish and tuna escape those deadly lines. The rope had marred her pale skin with angry-looking welts, and small blue bruises covered her hips.

Pointing a webbed finger at her waist, he sent, *Why do you wear this?*

Her face flushed crimson, and she tugged helplessly at one of the knots. *It was a mistake.*

Her efforts made her breasts bob more furiously, and he fought to keep his cock contained within its sheath. *You wish it removed?*

Yes. She looked up at him with pleading eyes, and his attempt at cool objectivity melted.

Here. He located the knife he'd made from a large green piece of sea glass. Careful to face the razor-sharp edge away from her, he sawed the rope free and dropped it to the stony floor beneath the chair.

Freed of the device, she rose toward the sun-dappled canopy above them.

Snapping out a hand, he grabbed her wrist. He would not let her leave. Not so easily. She would abandon him eventually. That was inevitable. But before she did, he wanted to show her what it was to be a mate. What it was to be utterly controlled and owned, as he now was. He could control her but only beneath the water. As long as she was down here, she needed him.

He sent, *Why did you come to me?*

Her gaze returned to him, and once again a flush infused her cheeks. *It was an accident.*

This does not look like an accident. He pointed to the belt. *This was to tie you to the ocean. To bring you to me.*

She pressed her lips together, brow furrowing in pain. *No. That...* Her hands crept over her smooth belly to lace her fingers together. *I was trying to kill myself.*

He narrowed his eyes, gauging her sincerity. *Why would you want to die?*

Her shoulders slumped, her body sinking until her feet rested against the smooth stone floor. *It's a long story. A silly one. The weights were so I couldn't change my mind.*

Tell me.

I lost a baby.

Zantu's gills fluttered. Mermaids considered children a burden. Something to be abandoned along with their mates. Never did they grieve the loss of one. But Brianna wasn't a mermaid. Her thoughts pounded his mind in a wave of unfiltered longing.

He curled his tail around the back of her knees, drawing her toward him. *I'm sorry you are grieved.*

She brought her hands up between them to press stiffly against his chest, as if creating a wall, but didn't shove with any real force.

He embraced her, running his fingertips lightly up the smooth curve of her finless spine. Her heartbeat fluttered against his chest, and he was reminded of how fragile she was, especially here beneath the waves. *Please do not try to die again.*

Her stiffness eased. This close, he could smell her unique, sunshine-dappled-waves scent. Her skin slid like silk against his, and his sheath pulsed with his cock's desire.

Closing his gills, he gathered air at the back of his throat and lowered his face toward her neck. He pursed his lips and gently blew a stream of bubbles against her collarbone. She shuddered, surprised enjoyment vibrating through their thought connection. Encouraged, he added sound, a baritone come-hither call that should penetrate her very bones.

She threw her head back, hips thrust forward, and he took the opportunity to slide his fingers over her folds, discovering her clit waiting like a little clam. Her heat intensified at his touch, urging him to increase his rhythm. He pressed against her slickness and caressed the nub until it swelled and pulsed with fervent need.

Her hands slipped from his chest to wrap around his ribs. Nipples hard as tiny shells crushed against his flesh, and she bucked against his fingers. His cock had sprung free now, bobbing in time to her rhythm, yearning for her each time her hip made contact with the tip. He gritted his teeth and continued rubbing, determined to make her come before he plunged himself into her heat.

A tiny squeak slipped past her lips in a stream of bubbles as her body shuddered in release.

I will make you mine. He thrust the thought into her mind even as he pulled her hips to him. Her legs spread wide, allowing him entry, and he pumped his tail to carry them both to the mossy bed. He wanted her beneath him, held in place so he could grind his hips against her. So he could know her full depths with every thrust.

She settled into the sponges and lifted her hips to meet his rhythm, tiny gasps sending bubbles from her mouth to tickle his cheeks. He dipped his head to claim her lips, his tongue probing one set of lips while his cock probed the other. When she came again, he clutched her rounded buttocks and pumped one final thrust into her core. His shudders matched hers, leaving him exhausted.

Wrapping his arms around her, he allowed himself to fall into sleep.

CHAPTER 5

*B*RIANNA WOKE TO groggy darkness. She stretched and rolled over to look for the bedside clock. Her movements were awkward, slow motion, unsupported. *What the...?*

Memories flooded back to her like a bore tide. The pier, the weighted belt, the water... the merman. *Merman?* That part must've been a dream, an escape for her mind before death took her. This must be death. She stared into the deep black, the weight of the entire ocean pressing against her. Nothingness. She hadn't thought it would feel so... alone.

A muscular arm snaked around her, and a voice sounded directly in her head. *Go back to sleep, my angelfish.*

She screamed—or squeaked, the sound muffled by water —and struggled free of the embrace. *Oh God, oh God, oh God.*

A short burst of sound, and the world ignited in lavender light. Zantu's webbed hands reached to still her. Blue-violet light reflected from his silver eyes and gilded his skin, accentuating the perfect muscles of his torso. *What's wrong?*

Her initial bout of terror was replaced by awe. The strange illumination came from everywhere and nowhere all at once, creating an eerie sort of moonlight without a source. And then there was the godlike form of the merman leaning over her, face creased with concern.

A soothing song pulsed from his throat, calming her nerves. Looking past him, she realized the water surrounding them was studded with what looked like tiny purple diamonds. *It's so beautiful.* She reached out to try to catch one of the motes, but it slipped through her fingers as if it were air. *What are they?*

Zantu wrapped his arms around her, nuzzling her neck and sending a stream of bubbles through her hair. *Humans call them plankton.*

Can you turn them on and off?

His chest vibrated with sound, and the water went black.

Oh, no, leave them on! She clawed forward, searching for him. Terror of the darkness, the unknown threatened to crush her.

You asked me to turn them off.

She located one of his biceps, wrapped both hands around it to pull him closer. *No, I wanted to know if you could.*

Again, he sang the motes awake, and Brianna looked up into a face full of amused tenderness that made her heart skip a beat.

He leaned in to press his forehead to hers. The odd-colored light made his eyes hard to read, but his voice in her head was full of all the sincerity she needed. *I will keep you safe. Always.*

She reached up to caress his cheek, enjoying the smooth skin along his angular jaw. God help her, she believed him.

At that moment, her stomach growled.

And I'll keep you fed. His chuckle matched the curve of his lips.

A craving for nachos filled her. Or maybe fried chicken. She licked her lips. What did mermen eat? Raw fish? She'd never been a fan of sushi. Even rare steak made her queasy.

Don't worry, little angelfish. We're mostly vegetarians. Sit. He pulled a chair away from the rosewood table and gestured.

So far, she'd only moved through the water with his aid. Now, left to her own mobility, she floundered over and took a seat. Luckily, he wasn't watching.

He'd taken a knife to the edge of the clearing and was cutting seaweed and other unidentified items, placing them into a huge half-shell bowl. She watched him work, the muscles of his back and arms bulging and rippling with his movements. His powerful tail flexed with muscle as well, each move through the water accomplished with mere flickers of effort. This had been her first chance to really look at him without him looking back. She wanted to reach out and touch the delicate-looking fin at the end of his tail. Examine what she imagined were tiny scales covering his body. Find out exactly where he hid his cock when they weren't making love.

I can show you if you like.

Her skin heated with embarrassment even as her pussy tightened. She'd forgotten he could basically hear her every thought.

He looked over his shoulder at her and winked. *Don't be embarrassed, little angelfish. I like to know what you're thinking.* In a flash of movement, he somersaulted through the water to face her and set the half-shell down on the table. *What do men look like in your world?*

Not like you. The tremor in her thoughts embarrassed her even more, but she refused to look away from him.

What's so different? He moved closer, hovering mere inches away, six-pack abs flexing with the tiny circular movements of his tail. His webbed hands spread across his ribs and slowly made their way down over his hips, drawing her gaze like a lure to the place where his cock should be—a bulge, there beneath the skin, covered as if by well-fitted clothing.

His thought reached out and caressed her. Compelled her. *Touch me.*

Swallowing, she reached out a hand and brushed her fingertips across the bulge. A note like a sigh of pleasure coursed through the water. Emboldened, she placed her entire palm over the lump, surprised by his heat. By the softness of his skin. She'd expected scales, but he was as smooth here as he was on his torso.

Scales are for fish. Desire colored his thought.

What are you, then?

Am I not a man?

She caressed the throbbing bulge, the crevice between her thighs immediately hot and slick. Fish or man, she wanted him.

Like magic, the skin beneath her fingers bloomed open to reveal a dark, throbbing cock. Her fingers squeezed the velvety hot thickness of him, coaxing a glistening pearl from the tip. Without thinking, she leaned forward and took him into her mouth. He tasted of salt and musk and every bit as male as any man she'd known.

He groaned, hands settling on her shoulders. *What are you doing to me?* His thought was thick with lust.

Delighted with the ability to "speak" while pleasuring him, she circled her tongue around the head of his dick. *Making you mine.*

His hands on her shoulders tightened. *Do not mock me.*

The urgency of his emotions touched her through their link like never before. Exposed and raw. His desire shone bright and full but was shadowed with a mix of anger and resignation she didn't understand. She wrapped her hands around his hips and pulled him closer to her, tilting her chin to take him more deeply into her mouth.

He groaned, his fingers digging into her shoulders as she sucked deeply. Against the back of her throat, she felt his release. After a shuddering moment, he disengaged and pulled her from the chair to squeeze her against his chest. *I will not let you leave me.*

The statement threw her off guard. Surprised her. She hadn't thought of escaping from Zantu, not since that awful episode with the mermaid. Despite the fact she was in the depths of the ocean. His promise to protect her made her feel safe. Nurtured.

He crushed his lips against hers. Her hands flattened against his ribs, her breasts tight against him, as he devoured her with deep, rolling thrusts of his tongue. If she'd been standing, she would've been weak at the knees. As it was, the water allowed them to twist and dance with each other without needing support.

His cock thrummed in a hard line against her belly, and she once again found his tail parting her legs. She slipped a hand between them, grabbed hold of him, and guided him inside her, yearning for the pressure of him, the fullness. The rippling muscles of his abs and the water slicking her skin ignited every nerve cell in her body with need.

Sliding a hand down her back to cup her ass, he pulled her firmly onto his rock-hard length and pressed himself into her core. He held there, deep and pulsing inside her while he ground against her clit. His tongue teased over her teeth and gums.

She wrapped her legs tightly around him, the edge of her climax rising above her like a wave about to engulf them both.

His teasing rhythm kept the wave hovering just out of reach. *You're mine.*

Please, please, she begged, unable to form a coherent thought.

Tell me you are. The hand on her ass squeezed, pressing him deeper into her folds with excruciating pleasure.

She threw back her head and bucked her hips against him, searching for release. *I'm yours. Please!*

Satisfaction dominated his thoughts, and he drew back only to pound immediately into her, again and again, until the wave broke and sent her spiraling into dizzying relief.

❦❦❦

BRIANNA'S HEAD thrummed with what reminded her of morning birdsong: trills from her left, bass-throated hoots from high to the right, and an eerie rising and falling tenor undertone she realized was coming from Zantu.

He sat on the shell-strewn floor at the edge of the clearing, tail curled to one side, as he appeared to be tending the fine fronds of bright-green eelgrass growing there. Sunlight cut sharp angles in the kelp swaying above their heads, filtering gold light down into the clearing.

Still not believing everything that had happened yesterday, she sent a tentative thought. *What is that noise?*

The ocean's salute to the sun, my angelfish. Come, breakfast awaits you.

She sat up, realizing he'd moved her to the bed some time during the night. Tiny bubbles rose from the sponges and caressed her sides. She stretched and looked around.

Her gaze fell on the table, where two bone china plates had been set along with what looked like two solid-gold forks. A half-shell bowl waited in the center, brimming with seaweed and whatever else Zantu had deemed edible, much of it floating free of the bowl but enough remaining within to be considered a meal. Her stomach quivered, still nervous about what he might consider tasty. But by now she was hungry enough to eat almost anything.

She pushed herself from the bed, aiming for the table, and discovered if she relaxed, she could walk, albeit in slow motion. The stones and shells beneath her toes were surprisingly rough, but solid enough to give her purchase, and she made it to the chair without floundering too much. She sat and admired the place settings.

Are those real gold? She reached for a fork.

They were my father's. Zantu joined her, sliding himself into the chair next to her. *He found them in a sunken ship many years ago.*

You had a father? The thought was out before she could think about how stupid she sounded. She covered her mouth, even though the words hadn't come from her lips. What a rude question. She'd never thought of mermen having families. Come to think of it, she'd never thought about mermen at all until yesterday.

Of course we have families. Well, fathers and siblings, at least.

Curiosity nibbled at her thoughts, and she fought to control it, but it was like only a sieve existed between their minds. *What about your mother?*

He used a smaller shell to scoop what looked like seaweed salad onto her plate, his thoughts obviously guarded. *Mermaids do not care for children.*

She frowned, unsure what to make of that bit of information. *So they have a baby and abandon it?*

He shrugged. *Fathers take care of the young.*

Are there a lot of other mermen? She looked around at the wall of kelp, as if the words might make one appear.

Zantu's hands paused briefly, then he pushed her plate in front of her, his silver eyes intensely regarding her. *Do not concern yourself with other merfolk.*

Brianna tilted her head, a small smile tugging the corner of her mouth. Was that jealousy she detected? *Afraid I'll run off with another merman? Or maybe a mer*maid—

Do not tease about such things.

The seriousness of his thought sobered her. Reminded her of her own vows of marriage, strengthened by her oath to her brokenhearted father to never follow in her mother's footsteps. She clenched her hands in her lap and stared at the seaweed salad. *I can't stay with you. I'm married.*

In your world, that means very little.

Her ire rose. *What do you know about our world? I take my vows very seriously.*

Even as she sent the thought, the hypocrisy of her words stopped her. The truth was, she'd abandoned her loyalty to Eric the moment she'd decided to jump. She'd chosen a coward's way out. And Eric was now as alone as her father had been. She might as well have divorced him.

Zantu placed a webbed hand over hers. *For a merman, a mate is for life.*

She looked at him out of the corner of her eye. *I thought you said mermaids didn't stick around.*

His jaw muscles twitched. *Even so, a merman will only ever take one mate.*

The way he thought *mate* held so much more meaning than could be put into words. Adoration. Certainty. Grief. And in spite of the contradictions, she knew exactly what it meant. The hopefulness of a word that could never truly be fulfilled. The inevitable loneliness of a life with the wrong person. Trapped in a marriage to a cold fish like Eric...

Her gaze shifted past Zantu's shoulder to the cradle resting in the middle of his nest. A baby cradle in a merman's lair. Had his mate left him with a child? Why else would he need a cradle? A twinge of jealousy invaded her as she pictured him with a gorgeous mermaid like the one they'd encountered yesterday. Then her gut squirmed. Why was she here? To raise a child in lieu of its missing mother?

A soothing series of notes permeated the water, stopping her thoughts. *Brianna, you are my mate.*

She met Zantu's gaze, blinking in confusion. *Me? What?*

You claimed me when you seduced me.

Seduced you? You're *the one who kissed* me.

The barbs of his dorsal fin darkened from blued silver to inky midnight. *I kissed you only to give you enough life to reach the surface. You're the one who... who... wrapped your legs around me and made me yours.*

Indignation drove her to her feet and sent her floating slowly upward. *Are you calling me a whore?*

He grabbed her wrist and pulled her back to the bottom beside him. His metallic-silver eyes bored into her with disconcerting intensity. *I don't know what a whore is, but from your tone, I believe it's a bad thing. So no, I will not call you a whore. But I don't want you to mistake my objective in saving you.*

Your objective? She tried to jab a finger toward him, her ire doubled by how slowly she was forced to move her hand. *You've made me a slave!*

We don't keep slaves. His grip on her wrist tightened, becoming almost painful. A series of deep clicks resonated through the water while his chest flexed widely like the hood of a cobra. *If anyone's a slave, it's me. I've avoided mermaid songs for thirty-five years, only to be captured by... by a human!*

She yanked her hand free of his grip. *If you feel that way about humans, why didn't you just let me die?* Even as she said it, she regretted it.

He blew a violent string of bubbles and rose to hover above the table. *Maybe I should have. But now I am bound to protect you. I could no more let you die than I could kill our child.* With a flick from his tail, he was next to the coral-supported cradle. *A merman's driven to nest, mate or no mate. To prepare. To care for a baby in spite of overwhelming heartbreak. When you have our child, I'll be ready to care for it, whether you're here or not.*

His words hit her like a rock skipped over the water, only sinking in after the momentum had played out. He'd said "our child." Could a human and a merman...?

I don't know. He responded to her half-formed question. *Mermaids carry half-human children. Abandon them with one mate or another. I imagine our union will produce the same.*

He spoke as if a child were a foregone conclusion. Could it be? Her fingers strayed to her abdomen. She and Eric had tried so hard... Her hands hooked into claws. She knew that wasn't true. Over the last twenty-four hours, she and Zantu had coupled more times than she and Eric had in the last two months.

The real question was not if it was possible, but did she *want* it to be possible?

Her gaze returned to the man before her. His silver tail brushed the pebbled floor while his torso glinted in the filtered morning sunlight. He was her mate. A mate for life. A mate who wanted children, had sworn to protect her, and had created a love nest for her before he even knew who she was. Leaving him would be the biggest mistake of her life. She walked toward him, attempting to be graceful in spite of the water's resistance. *Do you want one or two?*

A jolt of elation reached her through their bond—a bond she now recognized as special. The kind mates should have. He drifted to meet her, his silver eyes alight with fire. *As many as you will give me.*

She threw her arms around him and kissed him.

CHAPTER 6

ZANTU CRADLED HIS mate in his arms after making love again, free-floating in the center of the clearing. She rolled over to snuggle her back against him, and he flexed his tail to maintain contact around her bottom and legs. *You've curled up like a little shrimp,* he teased.

Through the mental connection, she huffed indignantly. I'm not sure I'll ever get used to floating around all day. Can we go lie on the bed?

He pushed her hair aside to dot tiny kisses behind her ear. Mmmm, I just realized you have something to offer no mermaid does. He slid one hand along her spine and cupped her bottom, fingers following the crease to discover her still-slick opening. We can do it from behind.

Brianna stiffened, her skin trembling with tiny vibrations. Fear, not excitement. He halted his caress. *Does that position offend you?*

Are you sure I shouldn't concern myself with other merpeople?

The worry he'd made a faux pas suggesting a new position was flushed away in a brine of adrenaline. Already she was thinking of other men. Yet her thoughts weren't full of lust... *Why do you ask?*

I think there's someone watching us.

Releasing his embrace, he whipped around in front of her, eyes scouring the kelp wall she'd been facing. Had Loia tracked them down after all? When his vision revealed nothing, he loosed a sonic query, reading the bounce-back for any irregularities. He knew this kelp forest like he knew his own fins.

A flash of turquoise silver caught the edge of his song. Familiar colors. Familiar shape. The tension in his shoulders and dorsal fin relaxed. He sang a playful coo, an invitation. "Ebby, come out."

From the floor between two crustacean-covered rocks, a tiny face appeared. "Hi, Uncle Zantu."

"What are you doing? Where's your father?" The sonic query should have revealed the larger shape of the merman or at least elicited an answering song. Perhaps his brother had spotted Brianna and fled.

The merchild remained partially hidden in the rocks, large eyes even more gigantic as they rested on Brianna. "What's that?"

Of course the child would be frightened, and Brianna's thoughts weren't exactly calm at this moment, either. He pulled his mate from behind him by the hand, singing and thinking at the same time, "Ebby, this is Brianna, my mate. Brianna, meet my nibling, Ebby."

Ebby slithered out from between the rocks, mottled turquoise skin shifting to blend with the darker greens and purples of the mussels behind.

Oh my God. A baby. A real live mer... what are merchildren called?

That. Merchildren. Zantu smiled.

Snagging the bit of silk from the cradle and wrapping it about her hips, Brianna approached the child clumsily and settled to her knees against the stone-and-shell floor. *Is it a boy or a girl?*

Merchildren are sexless until puberty, Zantu sent, only half-listening to her. Ebby was far too young to be wandering the kelp alone. Where was Rubac? Had something attacked his brother's nest?

"Now you'll be broken like Dad?" A thumb crept into the child's mouth.

Zantu ignored the unintended barb. "Where's your dad?"

"With the new baby. I'm hungry."

What's it saying? Brianna's undercurrent of thoughts thrummed with eagerness to touch the child, but she held back. Which was good. Merchildren were wary of females. He didn't need Ebby fleeing into the kelp. He made the effort to think as well as sing his interactions with the child.

"New baby? So Didra's there?" Mermaids often arrived at a mate's nest pregnant, seeking a safe place to give birth before wandering off again in search of more lustful prey. And mermen, in spite of themselves, lived for those gestational interludes.

"No. She left." Ebby's song shifted to a higher key of worry. "Now Dad won't get up, and I'm hungry."

Dread filled Zantu's chest. Mermaids might not be the best mothers, but they stuck around to nurse their newborns for a few weeks, at least until their mates had lined up a local sea lion or otter mother to provide milk. If Didra had split early, Rubac would not only be fighting depression, but struggling to feed a new child. Entire merfamilies had met their end for this very reason.

"Brianna, Ebby's hungry," he both said and sent the thought. "Would you mind getting some food?"

While Ebby followed Brianna to the table, Zantu patrolled the edge of the clearing, sending a long-distance note to his brother to ask if he was okay. No answer echoed in return, so he called upon the nearest señorita fish to carry a message that Ebby was all right.

Ebby's high-pitched protest drew his attention to the table. "I said don't touch me!" The spines on the child's dorsal fin splayed like sharpened claws, and the mottled turquoise tail had darkened to gray.

Brianna held one hand out, thoughts full of curiosity, acting as if she hadn't heard. *Your tails can change color?*

The child's angry. Zantu propelled himself over and put a hand over Brianna's. He should have warned her to keep her distance. "Ebby, calm down. She didn't mean anything."

I didn't mean to cause trouble. Brianna clasped her hands in her lap.

"Is she deaf?" Ebby backed toward the kelp.

"No," Zantu made a point of both speaking and thinking the words. "She's a human and hasn't yet learned our language. Why don't you help me teach her? She won't touch you again, I promise."

Ebby paused.

"Let's start with your name." He looked at Brianna and pointed to the merchild, saying, "Ebby."

Brianna made a face and recoiled slightly. *You want me to sing?*

Like this. Taking her hand, he pressed it to his breastbone. The note vibrated from him once again.

Wrinkling her nose, Brianna opened her mouth and emitted a pathetic trickle of noise.

Ebby giggled.

I can't sing. Brianna crossed her arms and slumped in the chair.

Pull from here. His hand brushed Brianna's nipple as he sought a spot below her breastbone, and he had to force-fully redirect his thoughts to the task at hand. Her enjoy-ment of his touch filtering through their mental connection didn't help.

With an inner sigh, she sat up. This time her sound was a bit stronger but still pitiful and far off-key.

He joined Ebby in laughter while Brianna glowered. *You just asked a starfish to rub your belly.*

I told you, I can't sing.

You just need practice. Try to make it lower, he thought, again repeating Ebby's name.

Squaring her shoulders, she let out a long grunt that rose and fell.

"Oh!" Ebby dashed to the nearby rocks and disappeared.

Zantu swallowed back dismay. "You just tried to summon a school of barracuda."

Fear laced through the thought connection, and she clung to his arm, looking around. *I did?*

"There are none nearby, thankfully." How could this be so difficult? Ebby's name was an easy note. A baby name. He throttled his thoughts, hoping none of his frustration leaked through. "Ebby, come out. There's no danger."

"I want to go home."

"I know. I'll take you soon."

"I can go myself."

"I don't want you out there alone."

What's the child saying?

Ebby's small quick form was already darting away, keeping low to the rocks.

"Ebby!"

The child's trickle of sonic guidance clicks faded in the distance. The child should not be roaming the forest alone. And then there was Rubac's condition to consider. And a new baby. Zantu needed to be sure everyone was all right.

He turned to Brianna and caressed her cheek with his fingertips and leaned in to brush his lips against hers. *I need you to stay here. I must check on my brother.*

Can't I come? I'd love to meet him.

Mermen do not bring their mates to another's nest. It's forbidden.

Why?

I don't have time to explain. You must trust me.

Before she could argue more, he slithered between the kelp toward his brother's nest.

⋖⋖⋖

BRIANNA HOVERED in the nest's gentle current, unsure what to do next. She hadn't been able to follow Zantu's conversation with the child, but she could only assume the merchild was in danger. Their singing exchange had sometimes contained notes barely within range of Brianna's hearing, and she wondered if there were other notes she hadn't heard at all. She'd tried to send her thoughts to the child the way she did with Zantu, but there'd been no response. Then she'd wondered if maybe they had to touch each other first. Bad idea, apparently. And now her tone-deaf singing had driven the child off for good. She prayed Zantu found Ebby before anything bad happened.

To kill time, she explored the clearing, admiring the way he'd integrated human items with ocean-based needs. The sea sponges for a mattress, the mother-of-pearl inlays on wood. When she bored of that, she tried to nap, but without Zantu to be her anchor, she felt exposed. Alone.

She was on the bottom of the ocean. Naked except for the scrap of silk she'd pulled from the cradle. At least she didn't need air. For how long? She wished she'd asked him.

From beyond the thick kelp wall, a constant humming and chirping reached her, as if she were in a forest full of birds and insects. She supposed the fish and crustaceans were the birds and insects of the ocean.

Curious, she put a hand through the fronds and pushed them aside, as if peering through curtains. A bright-orange fish met her gaze, seemingly as curious about her as she was of it. It wriggled there, looking at her expectantly. *I don't have any food for you, little guy.*

A mottled brown-and-white fish with a spiky dorsal darted up and nipped at the orange one.

Hey! Be nice!

The mottled fish darted side to side then hovered in front of her face, bulbous eyes moving independently of each other to look everywhere but at her.

The small orange fish returned, this time with a friend, and once again the brown fish shot out to attack it. The orange fish let out a pitiful cry, and Brianna found herself pushing through the kelp to come to its rescue. *Stop it!*

All the fish scattered.

Clear of the nest's confinement, she took the opportunity to survey the kelp forest. A rock wall covered with vibrant purple-and-pink mossy growth drew her attention. Unable to resist, she floundered forward to take a closer look. The wall teemed with fish and other creatures. A purple-speckled octopus bubbled out of a crack in the rock to slither down the wall and away as if indignant about her visit. A golden-shelled snail plodded a trail over an outcropping while small red shrimp darted across the surface around him. *You know how clumsy I feel in the water, I bet,* she thought at the snail.

Something stung her foot, and she jerked her knees up, realizing she'd stepped on an anemone. The sting burned like crazy. She grabbed her foot to look at the red welt striping her ankle. Twisting to keep from touching another anemone, she flapped her arms and legs and managed to gain some altitude. Without Zantu here, it seemed her body naturally wanted to be on solid ground rather than float. She'd have to pay better attention.

A small shark zigzagged by, startling her. She gulped, wondering if there were any larger ones lurking about. Putting her back to the wall, she decided she should return to the nest. Plus, her foot hurt like crazy.

She spun to retrace her steps and realized she wasn't entirely sure how. Layer upon layer of kelp all looked alike. How far down the wall had she travelled? *Stupid Brianna. He told you to stay put.*

The mottled fish with the dorsal fin nudged her hand. She pulled away, regarding it. After the anemone, she was extra cautious. But it merely hovered there, eyes rolling every which way as if it were a sentinel tasked to guard her.

Maybe she could find the crack with the octopus again and go from there? She fluttered her legs in that direction, limbs growing tired from the effort of staying off the bottom. What she wouldn't give for a life vest right now.

She glanced at the canopy above. If she surfaced, would she be able to breathe air again? And if she did, would she lose her ability to breathe water? She could barely remember why she'd wanted to drown herself—was it only yesterday? Now she had a sea god for a lover. A mate. She could imagine eternity, safe in his arms. And why not? Eric already thought her dead. Going back would solve nothing. She'd been given a new chance at life. At love. And, perhaps, at motherhood.

She kicked her legs again, searching for a familiar landmark along the wall. What if he never came back?

She banished the thought. He had to come back. They were mates. Of one mind. The missing mental connection felt like a hole inside her. Out of curiosity, she mind-called, *Zantu?*

Only silence.

Overhead, the curious orange fish appeared again, as if inviting her upward. Was it singing to her? Maybe she should swim up to the top of the wall and get a better vantage point.

She kicked her legs, propelling herself upwards with none of the grace Zantu could call upon. The mottled fish followed her, keeping close to her left ear, its song a funny little cicada buzz.

At the upper edge of the rock, the current grew stronger. She kicked harder, trying to keep close to the wall. The kelp forest up top was impossible to see through, but she thought she saw something move. Something large. Sharks returned to mind, and her heart accelerated to dizzying speed. She stopped kicking and allowed herself to sink again. She should just return to the seafloor and walk along it like before, sea anemones or not. Up here she felt out of control.

A broken leaf spun through the current and caught her across the cheek to flap over one eye. She clawed it away. When she could see again, the mottled fish was no longer in sight. Kelp fronds bumped her legs, grabbing her as she struggled against the current. The more she kicked, the more tangled she became.

Panic seized her. She thrashed against the restraining strands. While the kelp held her legs, the current continued to push against her torso, and she found herself lying on her back, staring at a wave-tossed slice of blue sky. Leaves covered her eyes, bound her right arm to her side, locked her legs in place.

What sounded like a laugh reached her, but she could no longer see. Without thinking, she screamed, the sound rising from deep in her gut. She knew it was louder in her head than in the water, but what if she'd just called another school of barracuda? Or a shark?

She clamped her lips together and sent, *Help!* with all the force she could muster. *Zantu, help!* How was he going to find her, so far from where he'd left her?

Water stung her eyes and nose. The kelp felt like it was crushing the breath out of her. She struggled against her bonds, wondering if she'd die down here after all.

CHAPTER 7

ZANTU FOUND RUBAC lying on a mound of sea sponges, a newborn curled on his chest. The nest was a more traditional merman's nest, with none of the human detritus Zantu loved to collect, other than the toys he brought for Ebby. The merchild was already there, glowering from behind a dollhouse.

"Brother?" Zantu approached the prone merman through a seaweed garden eaten down to stubble.

Rubac opened his lime-green eyes. "You've come."

"Ebby showed up at my nest complaining about a new baby."

"Didra said she'd be back." His voice held a minor key that boded ill for any merman. "But I know she won't be."

Zantu wanted to find the golden-tailed mermaid and strangle her with her own yellow hair. "Need help getting milk?"

Rubac waved a limp hand heavy with rings and what he called his prayer bracelet through the water. "There's no point."

Zantu took a closer look at the baby. The tiny nub of a tail lay limp across his brother's chest. A shock of ebony hair floated loosely in the current. But skin that should be mottled with newborn color remained pasty. Had Didra left because the baby was dead, or was it the other way around? His chest ached at the loss. "Rubac, I'm sorry."

"Will you take Ebby for me?"

Zantu's throat tightened. Mermen were very good at deluding themselves that their mates would be back any moment. Good at focusing on the children she brought them, in spite of a broken heart. Until his heart had enough. And once a broken heart fell apart, there'd be no return. Zantu couldn't allow his brother to just give up. "Remember when Dad left you in charge while he went to find medicine for that cut on his tail? How it felt to think he might not come back, and how we'd gone searching for him? Don't you think Ebby would do the same?"

"I knew he'd come back. I just wanted to go exploring." Rubac's mouth twitched upward, as if he wanted to smile but couldn't.

Sweeping the floor with his tail, Zantu kicked a flurry of small shells and debris at the merman. "I'm serious. Think about how we felt. You want Ebby to feel like that?"

Rubac's reply held a key of despair. "I need you to help so I can try to elevate the baby's soul."

If Zantu's throat had been tight before, now his entire chest felt as if it were about to cave in. His brother's love of mer-myth and magic could sometimes be entertaining, but in this case, it would likely prove deadly. The myth of elevation said a great blue whale could free a mer-soul from the cycle of the sea. But blue whales only lived out in the wild deeps, far from the safety of the kelp forest. Zantu and his brother had braved it several times before

Ebby was born, Zantu seeking salvage while Rubac spoke to the smaller whales and other creatures. Back then they'd had nothing to lose but themselves.

"Now's not the time to go chasing myths." He reached for the limp form on Rubac's chest. "Why don't I take care of the baby? You stay with Ebby."

Rubac's arm closed tighter about his dead child. "I have to try."

"A living child needs you. You can't take risks like we used to."

"That's why I need Ebby to stay with you."

"Ebby needs *you*, brother."

"You love Ebby, and you don't have a mate yet, so—"

"Uncle Zantu has a mate now," Ebby sang from behind the dollhouse.

The heart-wrenching drama with Rubac had almost made Zantu forget about Brianna. He hoped she wasn't too frightened. Although he'd verified no predators were near, every muscle in his body suddenly burned with the need to get back to her. Yet his brother needed him as well and just as badly. He was torn between two worlds.

Rubac rose from the mound of sponges and stared at Zantu. "You've been caught? When?"

"It's a long story, and I don't have time to tell it now. But I can't take Ebby. I need to know you won't abandon your child to pursue a myth."

"She's a human," Ebby threw out, holding up a long-legged, naked doll. "No tail."

Rubac blinked, frowned at the doll. He turned again to Zantu, his lime-green eyes now shrewd with curiosity. "Human?"

"I told you, it's a long story." Zantu pulled away, relieved by his brother's apparent return of clarity. "She's waiting for me at my nest."

"Waiting? Oh, you *have* been deluded." Rubac put a hand on Zantu's shoulder. "I'm so sorry. I thought you might be one of the lucky ones and escape the bond."

"Human women are different."

"You're serious." Rubac settled back onto the sponges. "You've bonded to a human."

"Indeed."

"I want to hear all about this."

His brother's innate curiosity gave Zantu a bargaining chip. "Promise you won't abandon Ebby and head off to the deeps, and I promise to come back in a day or two and tell you."

Rubac seemed to think for a moment then nodded his head. "I won't abandon Ebby."

Zantu blew out a string of relieved bubbles. Once he was more secure about leaving Brianna in the nest, he could come back to fulfill his promise. "Thank you. I need to get back to Brianna. She's never been alone." He pushed aside the screen of kelp to exit the clearing. "Remember your promise. I'll see you in a few days."

"You too, brother. Good luck."

Zantu slipped through the stalks, relieved by his brother's return to his senses. At least he hoped Rubac was okay and wouldn't abandon Ebby for a myth. But Zantu had other responsibilities than his brother right now.

ZANTU SENT OUT A THOUGHT, unsure how far the link might travel. He'd lost contact not far from the nest.

Nothing.

The brown-spotted sculpin he'd left to watch her was supposed to come find him if there was trouble. Not the best guard fish but more reliable than the capricious orange garibaldi fish who often served mermaids just for fun.

He jetted through the kelp, pulsing his sonic query ahead to clear the way. The kelp thinned as he exited Rubac's territory and reached the ledge down to his own. He jackknifed over a lip of rock, shooting straight for his nest.

Shoving through the thick wall of kelp into the clearing, he smiled in anticipation. He'd never had a mate to come home to before. Inside the nest, he looked around, and his smile faded. *Brianna?* She was nowhere in sight. He added a sonic query.

Gone.

Of course she'd left him. That was what women did. He'd hoped a human would be different, but obviously not. Why would he believe she was any different from any other female? Yet a dark cloud of doubt enshrouded his soul. His nest was far from land. How could she expect to strike out on her own and reach safety? There were predators, riptides, mermaids, and other dangers. Without fins or tail she'd be at the mercy of the current. He had to make sure she was safe, even if she had left him.

He slid out of the nest and searched for the sculpin guard. Missing, of course. Creating a song for the simple creatures in the area, he asked the whereabouts of the human. As one, the creatures pointed toward the rock wall nearby. An orange garibaldi giggled and darted away, trailing a few friends.

A flutter of panic leaked through Zantu's mind. He darted after the garibaldi through the rocks and between kelp, calling ahead with both mind and sonar.

Even with the current, she shouldn't have drifted far. Where was she?

A brown-speckled sculpin poked its head from behind a sea fan on the floor, its mind relaying the feel of rising toward the surface and the pull of the stronger current. Sculpins were bottom dwellers, and the creature's own instincts had overridden the directive to watch Brianna.

Zantu should have known better than to trust a sculpin to report trouble. Cowards, every one.

Another panic wave rippled through Zantu. Was the feeling his own or something he was receiving from Brianna? Speeding toward the surface, he called with both voice and mind. *Brianna!*

The panic in his chest grew stronger, and now he recognized it wasn't all his. A word whispered through his mind. *Help!*

Brianna! Where are you?

As he entered a thick section of kelp, the words grew stronger. *I can't breathe. God, hurry!*

He spun in place, searching the surrounding forest. He could detect nothing awry. The mind connection gave him no sense of direction. *Can you sing to me? Call me!*

No! There's something nearby. I'm afraid. The kelp— her thoughts were muddy, but the panic remained sharp and clear.

Summoning a song deep in his core, Zantu formed a command to every creature within range. "Protect my mate!"

The water churned with activity as nearby creatures passed the message along: low foghorn calls from a nearby black jewfish, buzzing from a school of perches, and low against the ocean floor, the ba-ba-ba of a few sea bats. And then a high bark from a sea lion, a warning about invasion of territory. Zantu homed in on the call, racing between the stalks until he spotted the whiskered face of the local sea lion male. He'd interacted with the creature before, and it tolerated Zantu in what it considered its domain.

"What is it?"

The sea lion bared its teeth with unusual aggression and responded with the note sea lions used to warn competitors away.

Zantu tilted his head to look out of the corner of his eye submissively. "You know me, brother. I'm not here to hurt you or your family. I'm looking for a human."

The beast circled him, the whites of its eyes showing starkly against sleek brown fur. It grunted a story about a mermaid playing games, using the kelp to trap and drown his harem's babies.

Stomach churning, Zantu ground his teeth. A mermaid would find Brianna even more fun to toy with than baby sea lions. "Take me there."

The big animal somersaulted once and shot through the kelp to an area shorn from its holdfasts to create a floating mat of greenery. Thick stems tangled in the canopy, yanking more stalks loose as the current continued its relentless path. In the distance, the shouts of the sea lion's harem met the taunting giggles of a retreating mermaid. The big male bellowed and sped in that direction.

Zantu coiled himself to follow then spotted glints of skin amidst the tangle of kelp. A naked foot peeked from within the mat. Realigning his trajectory, he tore through the mass toward his mate.

I'm here, he thought as he yanked the stalks and debris free. Pushing aside mats of flat leaves, he searched for her face.

Her thoughts had drifted into a hazy calm. Almost nonexistent. He tore a leaf aside and found her eyes staring at him. Through him. *No!* Immediately, he placed his lips over hers and released a stream of bubbles into her mouth. *Brianna, breathe!*

Her body bucked, the kelp still binding her limbs. She couldn't die. Again he kissed her lips, trying to recall exactly how he'd done it when they'd first met. It was one thing for her to leave him, return to the surface. Go back to her life there. Knowing she lived, he, too, could live on. But if she died in his arms, he'd have nothing to live for. *Please, Brianna. I love you.*

Free me, she thought.

The ache in his gut twisted sharply. Wrenched him to the core. Reminded him she'd left the nest, swum to the surface to seek escape. Even now, she sought to be free of him. He wished he could mimic that desire. The bond he'd thought to find a way to break had only strengthened as time passed. He was as trapped by the bond as she was by the entangling kelp.

Clawing at a handful of stalks, he tore them loose. Another handful. Unleashing himself on the inanimate plant matter, he shredded away thick stems and fronds and let them drift away on the current. "You shouldn't have left me," he growled, his thoughts a boiling stew of emotion she probably couldn't decipher. He wasn't even entirely sure what he felt except that it hurt beyond anything he'd ever thought possible. He wanted to hurt her and hold her at the same time.

The moment he jerked the last bond free, she wrapped her arms around him and buried her face against his shoulder. *Oh, God, thank you.*

His frenzied emotions dissolved like salt in water. Embracing her, he savored the feel of her warmth against him, the sunshine scent of her skin that had so captivated him. How could she hold such control over him? It didn't matter. He was hers, now and forever. And she was alive.

Don't leave me again. She gripped him tighter.

She was toying with him, of course. Using him when she needed him only to throw him away the next chance she got. His chest ached, as if the mate-bond might squeeze the life out of him. He tried to read her thoughts, but his own were too stormy to see past. *I thought you wanted to be set free?*

I wanted free of the kelp. *Did you think I meant free of you?*

Why else would you have tried to reach the surface?

She pushed away from his chest to look into his face. *I didn't. You were gone so long, and I got bored. There were these fish fighting, and I thought I'd break it up. I know it was stupid. I should have stayed put. The current sucked me away. I couldn't find the nest again. Then I hit the kelp and, and—* Her thoughts catapulted over one another, saturated with raw terror. *I thought I was going to die.*

A wave of relief rolled over him. And guilt. The connection of their thoughts couldn't lie. *I promise never to leave you alone again.*

He curled his tail up to caress the sensual curve of her bottom with his fin. Her legs still fascinated him, and the way she could embrace him with both her arms and legs during lovemaking drove him mad with lust. She sighed within her mind at his caress and spread her thighs. Her mind radiated trust. Commitment. Love?

His cock bulged and thrummed against its sheath, demanding release, demanding the satiation of her heated core, but he held back. He wanted to savor every moment he could. To make her want him as badly as he wanted her. He roamed his hands along the curve of her hips, thumbs grazing the slight hollows of her hip bones until they found the downy mound of fur between her legs. So soft, so hot, the mound pulsed as he cupped his fingers over it, slipping between those sensual legs.

She traced her hands over his arms, up his biceps, around his neck. He dipped his head to kiss her, fingers massaging her labia even as his mouth plied her lips open to receive his tongue. Her fingers reached the top edge of his dorsal fin and traced both sides of it down his spine to his hips. His cock sprang free. Still he ignored it, enthralled by the erotic gyrations of her hips against his hand.

Leaving her lips, he found a breast, taking her nipple between his teeth to nibble gently. Her fingers clawed into him, her mind spiraling with both pleasure and pain. He'd need to be cautious using his pointed teeth against her tender skin. Still massaging her slick nub, he moved to the other breast and drew the nipple to a barnacle-hard peak before tracing kisses along her belly.

She bucked and strained against him. He wrapped his other hand around to cup her ass and dipped his head between her legs to replace his fingers with his tongue. She tasted as good as she smelled, and bucked harder against him, her thoughts yearning for penetration.

As you wish, he sent, and plunged a finger into her. Her interior ridges quivered around his finger. He slipped a second inside and discovered that crooking his fingers while plunging her depths sent her into a cascade of pleasure. The shared mental connection to her shuddering climax nearly had him spilling his seed into the surrounding water.

Keeping hold of her sides, he slid up her length to find

her mouth with his again. His cock entered her core as easily as an eel returning to its den, smooth and graceful and a perfect fit. She sighed in mental satisfaction and lifted her face to kiss him.

I love you forever, he thought as he sent his seed deep within her.

CHAPTER 8

*L*IKE A BABY otter, Brianna lay atop Zantu's chest, while yards below them the kelp canopy undulated in deceivingly benign patterns. She reached up and broke the water's surface with one hand, the droplets on her fingertips refracting the setting sun into tiny rainbows. Drawing her hand back into the ocean's embrace, she ran her fingertips along the rippled muscles of Zantu's abdomen. The thought of going back down through the kelp to his nest terrified her. Being apart from Zantu terrified her. Everything about this ocean terrified her. More than terrified her. As both adrenaline scare and coital passion subsided, she realized she was angry as hell. *How could you leave me alone like that?*

Zantu hugged her closer, his tail rhythmically sweeping the water. *I'm sorry—*

She shoved at him, flailed as he released her, then clung to him and pounded his rock-hard chest instead. *What if you hadn't made it back in time? Did you realize I'd stop breathing?*

I left a sculpin to watch over you—

A fish? You left me in the care of a fish?

A mistake, I admit. He grabbed hold of the fist she'd been pounding against his chest. *I don't know why you had trouble breathing. The breath bond is supposed to last until the new moon. Perhaps that mermaid broke it.*

A new fear took root in the pit of her stomach. *Breath bond? Is that a spell? What if it gets broken again?*

I won't leave you again. His face was hard with resolve. *Not until I know how to keep you safe.*

His evasive answer shifted her fright into suspicion. *That's not what I asked.*

As long as I'm near, I can renew the bond.

She stared upward at the darkening sky. *You can't possibly guarantee you'll be at my side every moment of every day.*

His mind was a maelstrom of ideas until he settled on a tentative thought. *My brother might know of deeper magic.*

Her fist tightened beneath his palm until her nails dug into her flesh. *I'm not letting you leave me alone again.*

No. I won't do that.

What then? she asked, hoping mermen had some way to communicate over long distances yet knowing they didn't. If they had, he could have simply called his brother the first time.

You'll come with me. In spite of the wall he'd tried to erect between their mind-connection, horrific images flashed across her vision. A frenzy of mermen tearing one of their own limb from limb. Blood filling the water. Horrific silence as they departed, leaving the dead to feed the fish.

She gasped, salt water catching in her throat. *Who are those mermen?*

Zantu's chest rose and fell in a sigh. *Remember I told you taking a mate to another's nest is forbidden? The punishment for breaking the pact is death.*

Her heart was beating so fast she thought it might explode. *But... even your brother?*

My brother's not like other mermen. He'll hear me out. The words he sent were steady, yet she could detect a falseness to his confidence.

Why such harsh punishment? she asked.

Most mermen are solitary creatures, avoiding both maids and men alike. His arms tightened around her. *Unfortunately, weaker mermen have been known to indulge a mate's desire and reveal the locations of fellow mermen's nests. Any merman not mate-bonded would likely be forced to mate, no better than a slave. Any who rejects her faces her wrath, not only toward himself but also his children. Entire families have been destroyed by a single mermaid. A nest is supposed to be a sanctuary. A safe place, hidden among the kelp away from predators and mermaids. Revealing a nest's location is one of the gravest sins. Carrying out punishment is one of the few times mermen will gather together.*

She swallowed, unable to erase the violent images from her mind. *I don't want you to get hurt.*

Rubac and I share a special bond, closer than other brothers. We spent many years together exploring the wild deeps for treasure and knowledge. When Didra caught him I thought our relationship would end, but he's strong. He trusts me to visit his nest. To care for his child.

What if you left me at the surface? She squeezed him tighter, pressing her face against his chest. *I could tread water there and breathe until you got back.*

His already-dark thoughts became stormy. *The surface is not safe. Predators can see you from below, waves can bury you from above.* And other humans could find you and take you away.

He didn't say the last part, but it carried across his thoughts unbidden. She stroked her fingers along his dorsal lovingly. *I do not want to leave you, my love.*

A shiver passed over his skin, and guilt soured the mind-connection. *I'm trying to trust you. But all I've ever learned of women tells me otherwise.*

From what little she'd learned—and seen—of mermaids, she knew he was fighting an uphill battle. She wanted him to trust her. Believed he would in time. And she had to admit, the idea of fending off sharks or trying to keep her head above crashing waves sounded as unlikely as surviving a journey to Rubac's nest. *If the surface is out, there must be another option. Where'd Rubac learn about the magic? Can we go there?*

Bubbles streamed from his nose. *The wild deeps would be more dangerous than taking you to Rubac's nest. I think Rubac will understand the special circumstances. Especially since you've already met Ebby.*

Her thoughts returned to the merchild and the reason Zantu had left the first time. *Is Ebby okay?*

Ebby's safe for now. My brother's the one who concerns me. Zantu's thoughts blurred and wavered with uncertainty.

Why?

His new baby is dead. Most likely stillborn. He's...

Stillborn? The mind-connection with Zantu popped and seemed to fizzle, as if shorted out. An unexpected tsunami of memory slammed into her. The first sound of her baby's heartbeat. The smell of new paint in the nursery. The sensation of that first fluttering kick from deep inside her. And then the day she'd realized the kicking had stopped. The pain of fruitless labor and delivery. Blessed unconsciousness from blood loss.

And finally, Eric standing in the hospital doorway telling her he'd already "taken care of things." She'd been unconscious five days, and the ashes had already been scattered.

The sting of water in her nose and throat yanked her back to the present. Water squeezed from every side, forcing the breath from her body. She realized she was gasping, and there was no air to be found.

Zantu's hands grasped her face, and she felt his mouth against hers. Her lungs eased immediately. His kiss was tender, gentle. Infused with love rather than lust. An anchor in her storm. He tilted his head and traced kisses along her jaw, his hands stroking her back as if gentling a horse. *I believe I understand now why you came to me,* his mind whispered to hers.

She might not have a physical voice, but her thought was choked with pain. *He took her from me. I never got to say goodbye.*

I'm so sorry. He gathered her in his arms.

Maybe it was because of the mind-connection, but the genuine shared grief flowing from Zantu's thoughts was stronger than all the combined words of comfort she'd received from family and friends. Definitely more than she'd received from Eric, who couldn't understand why she wasn't grateful to escape the chore of a funeral. She broke down and sobbed against her mate, truly cried as she never could with Eric. Zantu held her tight, saying nothing, because he didn't have to. It was enough that he was with her. Enough that he wanted with all his heart to make things better.

She cried from the pit of her soul, and the ocean accepted her tears as its own.

❧❧❧

AFTER COMFORTING BRIANNA'S GRIEF, Zantu carried her through the night-dark kelp. Her thoughts were sorrowful but solid. Something inside her had changed, as if brackish water had been washed away by an incoming tide. She'd been through a lot—even before he'd met her. How lucky he was to have a mate who not only wanted to stay with him, but also wanted children. Children they would raise together. The anxiety he felt about approaching his brother's nest was caught up with a desire to share news of his lucky pairing. Who would have guessed a human would make such a perfect mate?

He pumped his tail and carried them toward Rubac's nest. Hopefully night would mask Brianna's proximity while he talked to his brother. Some silly part of him hoped he could get away without Rubac ever being the wiser about having his nest revealed. Another part hoped his brother noticed and wanted to meet his mate. He'd always wondered how a merman could be so weak as to take a mate to see other mermen, but now a part of him understood the draw of wanting to introduce your bond-mate to your brothers.

Brianna clung to his shoulders, thoughts numb with exhaustion. Adrenaline kept him moving. He sent sonic queries ahead to guide his path. A merman was never blind as long as there were landmarks for echolocation. One danger of the wild deeps was the vast expanse of water with nothing physical to orient himself with except the current. He prayed his brother had the answers they needed, because a trip to the wild deeps would be unthinkable with Brianna in tow.

He reached the thick wall of kelp surrounding Rubac's nest and unhooked Brianna's arms from his neck. Guiding her hands to a barnacle-rough stone, he thought, *Stay exactly here. I'll be just on the other side of this kelp. If I need to bring you into the nest, do not make eye contact. Do not interact. Most importantly, do not make physical contact of any sort. You saw what happened with Ebby. Pretend you're invisible, okay?*

She nodded into the darkness, which he felt as a slight ripple of water.

He stroked her cheek with his knuckles and then brushed her lips with his. She was too beautiful to ever be invisible, but his brother was already mated and should be immune to most female charms. Thinking of her charms ignited a fire low in his belly, and he had to rein back his desire. Now was not the time nor place.

Turning from her, he pushed aside the thickly woven kelp. Normally he'd have announced himself before entering, but he wanted to forestall Rubac's sonic query. Once Zantu was inside, Rubac's shorter query would hopefully miss Brianna's presence outside.

Moving past the kelp, he approached the mound of sponges Rubac normally rested on. He knew the layout from previous visits and moved with confidence to within an arm's length of the bed. "Rubac, it's Zantu."

No answer. Not even the shush of water against fin as Rubac or Ebby stirred.

"Rubac? Ebby?"

Still the clearing remained silent. He chirped another query and read the bounce-back. Nobody was home. He sent a louder query, verifying the other objects in the nest. Ebby's toys were right where the child always left them, and the mound of sea sponges was undisturbed. Nothing seemed out of place.

Zantu's heartbeat sped up until it pounded in his ears. Something wasn't right. He returned to where he'd left Brianna, relieved to find she was where he'd left her. *There's nobody home.*

Where do you think he went?

He rubbed a hand through his hair. All he could assume was that Rubac had taken the baby's body to inter it in the reef at the edge of the wild deeps. Why his brother had decided to do it at the edge of nightfall was a mystery. *Probably the baby's funeral.*

Oh. Her thoughts grew dark, her own loss a sharp background full of scars. *Shouldn't you be there, too?*

Her concern for his brother in spite of her own mental state touched him. *Funerals are rare, and very private when they happen. Most merfolk die in seclusion, and the dead are undiscovered until their bones have already scattered to the sea. When a loved one does find a body, it's taken to the edge of the reef and tucked into a crevice.*

The idea of Rubac at the edge of the reef, where the kelp dropped off and the wild deeps began, made Zantu nervous. Especially at night, when large predators rose to hunt. Ebby wouldn't be able to keep up the same pace Rubac did. The child would have to rest. Yet sleeping would be impossible with the current continually flowing out to the deeps.

He sent a long-range query through the kelp. A flutter of night-feeding damselfish but nothing else. The forest felt too quiet. He didn't like being outside the protection of a nest. *We'll wait inside. I imagine he'll be back in the morning.*

Won't he be angry to find us here?

Probably. But I'm not taking chances sleeping outside with you. He elbowed aside the kelp curtain and pulled her through. The current inside the nest was much weaker, and he relaxed his grip around her waist. *Do you want to rest on the bed, or would you prefer to float?*

Her fingers tightened around his forearm. *I can't see a thing.*

Exhaustion from the day's activities all seemed to drop on him at once, weighing him down like a bottle swamped with seawater. He could have called on the plankton to light the place, but it seemed easier to simply make the decision. *I think we'll rest on the bed tonight.*

He carried her to the tuft of sea sponges and relaxed, allowing their combined weight to settle them into the cushioning surface. Brianna turned to spoon herself into his embrace, her sleepy thoughts full of contentment, lulling him to sleep.

He murmured a lullaby into her hair, "You are my sunken treasure."

She sighed and snuggled closer. The gentle trickle of water over his skin soothed his sore muscles, and he fell into a deep sleep.

CHAPTER 9

RIANNA BLINKED AWAKE in the darkness but this time with no confusion or fear. A predawn chorus of fish played a soothing background melody, and she snuggled closer into Zantu's warm embrace. She was delighted to feel his morning erection pressing against her bottom. His mind was blank with sleep, his body hers to explore, so she reached a slow hand around behind her and sought the throbbing shaft that'd woken her.

Sequestered in its sheath, his cock responded to a little coaxing from her hand. He flexed his hips toward her but didn't waken. Keeping her mind purposefully blank so as not to wake him, she wrapped her fingers around his heated shaft and pressed her thumb over the small slit at its head. Her pussy tightened with desire as she imagined his cock inside her. Seeking lower, she found his testicles hiding within the sheath. She massaged the tender sack, rolling the orbs between her fingers.

Zantu pressed his hips harder against her and crushed her in the circle of his arms, not enough to hurt but enough to immobilize her. A low growl rose from his throat against her ear. *Good morning, my little angelfish. Or should I say devilfish?*

The vibration sent shivers deep inside her, creating an ache that needed to be filled.

His hand sought hers still wrapped around his cock, encouraged her to squeeze and press his shaft downward. The tip grazed her ass, and she rubbed herself over it. *Depths, woman. We're on my brother's bed.*

So?

He slid her higher along his body until her opening was poised directly over his cock, the head teasing her lower lips. Both his hands found her breasts, fingertips pinching her nipples until they stiffened.

She arched her back, thrusting her hips against him to take him in, but he resisted, keeping the tantalizing head just at the opening. He sent, *I want to kiss your lips.*

She started to turn, but he held her facing away.

Not those lips. He lifted her farther up along his chest, skin sliding against skin, strong hands guiding her by her hips. His chin grazed her spine, making her back tingle. When he reached the top of her buttocks, she felt his tongue caress the upper edge of her crack. Both his hands encircled her ass cheeks, spreading her wide. One thumb crept inward to circle her anus. She puckered, yearning for more no matter his intent.

Thumb massaging with gentle pressure, he slid his face lower. She gasped as he thrust his mouth between her legs. His tongue slipped along her quivering folds, ending at the throbbing nub of her clit. The pressure of his mouth sent shudders of pleasure deep into her belly.

At some point they'd floated above the bed and now free-floated in the water. She flailed, seeking something to grip, something to ground her as he worked the sensitive button of flesh with his tongue and teeth.

Hold onto your breasts, he commanded. *Pinch them for me.*

She clutched her own flesh, pinching until the electric jolts of sensation from his mouth met the matching ones from her nipples.

His mouth covered her pussy, tongue circling every crevice before plunging deeply into her. She arched, aching for more. *I need you,* she thought.

And then he began to sing.

The deep vibrations worked into her bones, filled her as surely as if he were fucking her. The sensation grew to enormous proportions, demanding release, and yet she yearned for the moment to last forever. Every muscle tightened, unable to escape his song. The thrumming, pulsing cadence worked her very core until the crescendo rolled over her in a great spasming release.

With a single purposeful move, Zantu pulled her down, and his cock settled deep into her folds.

She moaned, rising through another crescendo toward climax. His hands on her hips held her tightly against him, his body rocking hard. She widened her thighs and wrapped her calves around behind him, straining to take him deeper. She wanted his cock to touch her soul. To make him come so deep he melded with her forever.

A gasp left him as he clutched her tightly, driving his seed deep inside her.

Zantu startled awake to early pink sunlight reflecting through the kelp foliage above the nest. He'd fallen asleep almost immediately after making love, arms cradling his mate like a precious pearl. Wondering what had woken him, he gently released her and slid from the sponge bed. Rubac would have taken refuge during the night, but with morning light, he could return at any moment. Zantu hoped his brother never found out they'd made love in his nest, but even if he did, that moment with Brianna had been worth it.

The usual fish song trickled through the water, nothing apparently amiss. He didn't want to send a sonic query to Rubac and risk waking Brianna, so he decided to gather breakfast instead. The overharvested seaweed gardens would offer little for a meal, but Zantu didn't want his angelfish to start the day hungry.

Rubac didn't utilize human artifacts much, and Zantu had to search among Ebby's toys to find a beautiful cobalt-rimmed bowl. Taking the bowl to the outer edges of the garden, he searched for edible leaves and pods, leaving the newest seedlings in place for future meals. The garden was in even worse shape than he'd originally thought. How long had Rubac lain here grieving, leaving poor Ebby to fend for food alone?

He decided to take a quick patrol of the outer nest, both for food and to scout out anything of concern. Perhaps he'd find a clue about where Rubac and Ebby had gone. Much as he told himself things were probably fine, his brother's state of mind hadn't been exactly stable when Zantu had left him.

Outside the nest, sunlight danced and glittered across the forest floor as the current tossed the canopy above. A nearby garibaldi let loose a string of notes that sounded like rain against the water's surface. Farther out, a moray eel clacked its teeth before retreating into its den. Zantu found a small patch of red dulse and bent to pick the fronds.

Something brushed against his dorsal fin. He turned to find a small yellow señorita fish looking at him, its tiny mouth pursed as if it had something to say. "What is it, little one?"

"Sorry, brother," the little fish recited—señorita fish were excellent at parroting back a song. "Elevation called. Sorry, brother. Elevation called."

Zantu stared at it in shock. His brother had gone to the wild deeps anyway? What about Ebby? Depths. He must've taken the merchild along. The fish had been left as a messenger to Zantu in case Rubac didn't return. The fish darted into the kelp, job apparently done.

Dropping the bowl, Zantu raced back to Rubac's nest. Brianna rolled over at his arrival, stretching in a languid arch he didn't have time to appreciate. *I have to go after my brother. He took Ebby to the deeps.*

Why? She sat up to look at him.

There is a myth, a type of funeral called an elevation which can free a soul from the cycle of the sea. It can only be done in the wild deeps with the aid of an ancient blue whale. He went to her, taking her in his arms. He realized he'd never told her about the deeps, only sought to protect her from them. *The deeps are past the kelp forest, where the sharks and squid and other predators live. There are no landmarks to guide by, only the strength of the current, which can challenge even a merman's stamina. I can't take you there. And I can't leave you here.*

She grabbed his arms and pushed away from him. *What the hell are you suggesting?*

It dawned on him that he was suggesting releasing her. Setting her free.

Oh, no you're not. We're mates, remember? Whatever we do, we do together. Besides, land's in the opposite direction, and you don't have time to dawdle. I'm coming with you. Just give me a knife or something to help fend off the predators.

The determination in her thoughts about drowned him. He'd been trying to believe she wanted to be with him, but some part of him had been waiting to prove she was lying. That, like any mermaid, she'd leave him without looking back. But at this moment she was digging through Ebby's toys, looking for a weapon. Planning to accompany him on a journey that could kill them both.

Any reservations he may have had about her washed away.

Yet that knowledge didn't eliminate the problem at hand.

He searched through Rubac's small statues, jewelry, and other mythic artifacts but couldn't find anything that might serve as a weapon. Looking up, he saw Brianna brandishing a long pole with a net on it wider than his shoulders. *I can use this to push things away or tangle them up.*

In spite of the fear gripping his insides, he smiled. *My ferocious little angelfish.*

CHAPTER 10

ZANTU CLUTCHED BRIANNA tightly against his chest and exited the kelp forest. They'd been swimming for hours, heading toward the great chasm where predators hunted other predators, often merely for sport. The sudden lack of foliage, coupled with the immediate drop into nothingness, always made his stomach flip. His most recent trip to the deeps had been when he'd followed a trail of cargo containers washed overboard during the last autumn storm. Then, he'd run into a raven-haired seductress prowling the area and nearly lost his freedom. Now he'd be risking something much more precious.

He sent out a sonic query to test the dark waters. The song would not only provide him bounce-back information on what was ahead, but it would also frighten away any mindless hunting squid. Sharks and whales were another matter—much trickier to coerce—but he'd deal with them if the need arose.

How are we going to find them? Brianna asked.

He pointed to a dusky cloud of krill interrupting the milky light reaching from the surface. *See the krill? We look for that. Whales follow krill, and Rubac's looking for whales.*

He emitted a short burst of song, searching for the gigantic animals. Nothing.

I can't see anything. The tremor in her thought reflected his own nervous fear.

There's nothing to see. Whales haven't found this swarm yet. We'll keep looking.

He pressed onward, farther and farther from the safety of the kelp forest into ever deeper water. The true wild deeps didn't begin for another quarter league, where the colder waters from the north joined and pushed underneath the current coming off the kelp reef. He'd been down that current ages ago, when he and Rubac had first ventured out of their father's nest. They'd found their first sunken ship there, and Rubac had been introduced to the intelligent whales who carried the sea's myths.

"Sink you, Rubac," he muttered within his song. Would Ebby even be able to survive those cold depths? Would Brianna?

A drumbeat reached him from far ahead. Then a low moan dropped its pitch through the water.

Brianna's fingers dug into his shoulder. *What's that?*

He gave her a short squeeze of reassurance, his own pulse loud in his ears. *Blue whales.*

A warning thump beat the water as the whale sensed their presence. "Go play your games in another pool," the whale's ponderous voice cautioned. "You've caused enough trouble for one night."

Zantu slowed. "I'm not here for games. I'm seeking my brother and his child. Have you seen them?"

A dark form moved between them and the surface. Zantu kicked his tail to resist being thrust downward in its wake.

"Ah, merman," the whale grated, its barnacled body stretching forever into the darkness. "I thought you were a maid. Your females have delighted in inciting a frenzy among the nearby sharks."

Zantu resisted the urge to send a sonic query into their surroundings. Sharks were bad enough, but now he'd have to watch for mermaids as well. "Have you seen another male? He would have asked you to assist with an elevation."

The drumbeat sound approached again, and a great mouth, open as if to swallow them whole, appeared. "An elevation? How odd." The mouth brushed by, revealing the black orb of an eye, a dark moon to counter the pale sun outlined above the surface.

Brianna remained surprisingly calm in the midst of the inspection. Excited but not frightened, even daring to reach her hand out to brush the whale's scarred hide. *Can you understand it?*

The eye regarded them while the voice continued to groan through the water. "What's this? A human?"

Nerves jangling, Zantu thrust out his chest and swelled his song to potent volume. He wanted there to be no doubts about how far he'd go to protect the human at his side. "My mate."

The whale blinked and seemed to sigh. "I've not seen a mated human in over a century. You have much to learn. But now," the whale sang in a heavy tone, appropriate for a funeral, "I believe I hear your brother."

In the far-off distance, Zantu could barely detect the familiar notes of his brother's sonic query. The whale answered with a moan that seemed to shake the very ocean, and drifted off to swallow more krill.

"Rubac!" Zantu called, moving to intercept.

You've found him? Brianna clutched him with one hand, and the netted pole with the other, struggling to keep from losing it in the water's resistance.

Ahead.

They left the whale behind, Zantu querying madly to discover Rubac's location. His brother's song had stopped, but the higher, more uncertain chimes of Ebby's song grew louder. "Uncle Zantu!"

Zantu raced ahead, drawn to Ebby's voice. Finally, he saw Rubac's form.

Alongside the unmistakable curves of a mermaid.

Zantu halted his momentum. *The whale said there was a mermaid around.*

Oh shit. Brianna brandished her net in front of her, looking about. *I still can't see a thing.*

I don't see Ebby. A sonnet trilled to his left, accompanied by the notes from a fish-harp. He spun, only to spot the disappearing flash of an indigo tail. *Depths. There's more than one.*

He turned back toward Rubac and thrust forward, hoping to at least find safety in numbers. The mermaid teasing his brother had yellow hair and a golden tail. Didra.

"Oh, you've come to our party!" she chimed, clapping her hands. "Rubac's such a bore."

"Where's Ebby?" Zantu shouted. To his relief, the tiny figure materialized through the krill-speckled water. The child held back a distance, avoiding the mermaids and watching.

A duet behind him sent him spinning around in time to pull Brianna beyond the reach of a raven-haired mermaid. Her dark tail caught the light as she passed by, first iridescently green and then swirling violet. A section of her tail fin was missing, the jagged edge puckered with old scar tissue. She cooed, "I've heard about you, Zantu."

Her partner was familiar, nimble fingers plucking a fish-harp's tines. "Loia."

She laughed while her accompanying veil of fish shimmied and shifted around her in time to her harp. "I warned you a human was no fit mate for a merman. Especially a big strong merman like you. She'll never be able to keep up with our games."

Brianna's knuckles were white around the net pole, every muscle in her body tense. *What's she saying?*

Threats. Behind him, he heard the tiny susurration of skin against water as Didra shifted position. His brother remained eerily silent, eyes hooded, tail fin limp. There was no sign of the stillborn child. "Rubac? You okay?"

No answer.

The raven-haired mermaid swooped up from below, rubbing her scarlet nipples along Zantu's length. Brianna recoiled, arching away from the contact and throwing him off-balance, but he caught her and pulled her against him tightly.

An arm's length away, the mermaid backflipped to face them again and rolled a small dart between her fingers. Immediately, Zantu knew what was wrong with Rubac. Love toxin.

The mermaid's voice chimed with deceptive playfulness, her scarred tail fluttering with mesmerizing iridescence. "I wonder what would happen if I used this on her?"

He swelled his chest. "I will kill you if you touch her."

Brianna's thoughts spun like a water spout, her attention first on one mermaid then another. She poked the net at Loia. *We're surrounded.*

Fingertips tickled the tips of his dorsal fin, sending a shudder through his blood as Loia's lilting melody of desire began. "Oh, are we going to have fun now."

He twisted to bat the hand away. Loia's veil of fish enveloped them. Summoning his sonic blast, he sent them scattering. The scent of blood filled the water. Brianna's blood. He had to get her out of here. Get Ebby out of here. Fast. His brother... his brother would have to fend for himself. Coiling the muscles of his tail, he lurched forward between Rubac and his mate. "Ebby, swim home!"

Something nipped his side. For a moment he thought it was another of Loia's fish. He brushed a hand over the spot to flick it away and found the dart lodged there. Depths. He'd been hit with the toxin. Jerking it free, he continued his momentum, barely registering Ebby's tiny figure matching his pace several yards away. The fog of the poison was already taking hold. His muscles ached as he tried to force them to keep working. To get his mate to safety. The grip he held on Brianna slipped, her skin scraping along his side before he caught her again.

She clung painfully to his neck, her feet kicking in a pitiful attempt to help them swim. *Zantu, what's wrong?*

She hit me with a love toxin. Soon I'll be paralyzed. He didn't know what to do. His gaze scoured the blank expanse of water for anything, anywhere he could hide Brianna. His grip slipped again, and he realized his tail was twitching ineffectually against the current.

"Uncle Zantu, what about Dad?"

Sink it, Ebby was in danger here, too. Not from the mermaids—Didra wouldn't allow the others to harm her own blood. But she wouldn't ensure Ebby made it back to the safety of a nest, either. Ebby would be abandoned. "He'll be fine." He prayed he wasn't lying. "I'm going to be paralyzed soon, like him. You have to get back to the kelp forest. Take Brianna."

"I don't know the way."

He opened his mouth to tell the child how, but his voice had succumbed to the effects of the toxin. His arm now refused to keep hold of Brianna, and she clung to him as if he were a dead piece of coral.

Zantu?

You have to show Ebby how to get home. At least his mind-connection still worked.

How? I don't know the way, and I couldn't tell Ebby even if I did.

Keep the current to the right and in front of you. Stay out of the cold layer—it'll suck you to the bottom very quickly. If it does touch you, keep it hard to your right and swim upward as fast as you can. Ebby wriggled into view, turquoise eyes confused and frightened. He hoped somehow the merchild would trust Brianna.

The laughter of mermaids tinkled toward him like hail against the surface.

Kiss me, he thought.

What?

You have to let go now, and I want your breath-bond fresh. The thought of her drowning was almost as paralyzing as the toxin. All he could hope was that she broke the surface before the spell ended.

No! They'll rip you apart! The terror clawing through her mind was stronger than it had been while she'd been trapped by kelp.

If you don't, both you and Ebby will die.

Brianna's gaze cut to the merchild, then her lovely face crumpled in anguish. *I don't want to leave you.*

I know. He sought to make his thoughts calm. To reassure her. *But you have to. You have to save the child.*

She bit her lips together then nodded. Grief reddened her beautiful green eyes. Taking his face between her hands, she placed her soft lips against his. *I love you.*

The toxin didn't take away his ability to feel, only to move, and he was thankful in this instance to have one last memory of her. *And I love you, my angelfish. Now swim. Get back to shore if you can.*

She released him and turned to the merchild. Ebby's tail flashed with alarming colors, unable to settle on a single camouflage. The child's attention flicked to Brianna then back to Zantu. "I'll take care of her, Uncle Zantu."

Ebby reached out a tiny webbed hand and took Brianna's, pulling her away into the dark waters.

❮❮❮

BRIANNA GRIPPED Ebby's hand and kicked to assist their momentum. The mermaids' songs echoed through the water, trying to lure her back. She wondered if Ebby felt the pull, too, or if merchildren—being sexless—were immune. The possible biological reason for a merchild's androgyny made a lot of sense right now.

The song's pull doubled her reluctance to leave Zantu and forced her to use every ounce of will to keep moving away. If it hadn't been for the merchild, she would have stayed by her mate's side, fought each murderous mermaid with every ounce of strength left in her body. She prayed he could find a way to escape. To find her again. He was stronger than any man she'd ever met.

Ebby dragged her along, using the current to aid their momentum. Now it was time to turn against it. To head back to the kelp beds. Brianna pulled against the child's grip and pointed with her free hand into the distance, keeping the water's flow slightly to her right as Zantu had instructed.

Ebby's eyebrows rose at Brianna's nonverbal instruction. The merchild blinked twice then nodded and changed direction.

Brianna let out a sigh of bubbles, grateful the child wasn't going to argue. Zantu's last wish had been for Ebby to reach safety, and Brianna would do everything she could to make that happen, even if she drowned in the process. She kicked with all the stamina she could muster. But exhaustion was already setting in. The drag created from the net was stronger than she'd previously realized, perhaps because they were now going against the water instead of with it. Poor little Ebby wriggled ferociously, but it didn't feel like they were making much progress.

A cramp seized her right calf, and she doubled over, awkwardly trying to massage it without letting go of the net. The tiny teeth marks left by the mermaid's swarm of fish continued to trail blood.

Swallowing, Brianna searched the surrounding waters. Hadn't Zantu said something about predators? Once, she'd watched a nature show about giant squid, with green-and-black video of a man-sized creature latching onto a diver's faceplate. The scrape and crunch of its beak biting the plastic still resonated in her memory. Zantu'd used his song to check for predators, yet Ebby moved through the water silently. Brianna hoped it was another survival trick, like the androgyny that made them immune to mermaid songs.

Overhead, the sun's orb seemed weaker, and the water had grown decidedly cooler against her skin. She reoriented toward the surface and aimed the net like a prow. Her leg threatened a new cramp, but she persisted in kicking until Ebby noticed and shifted direction. The downward pull was even more relentless than the outward current, and it seemed forever until a sudden flush of warmer water gave Brianna an extra burst of energy. She kicked like mad toward the sun.

Suddenly Ebby froze and spun to look behind them. A tremble passed between their connected hands, and Brianna squinted into the dark. Shadows. Moving shadows. Had the mermaids found them? The sharp curve of a dorsal fin cut through the waters.

Sharks.

Seriously? Sharks? She felt like she was playing a part in

the worst horror movie ever. She clutched the net tighter, realizing how silly and useless a thing it would be.

The creatures moved sinuously toward her, toothy mouths open to taste the water. A large one was in the lead. When a smaller one moved abreast, the giant shot sideways to bite at it. Another midsized shark passed the fight, dead set on engaging its prey.

For the first time, Ebby let loose a wide arc of sound. It was nowhere near as authoritative as Zantu's thunderous voice, but it still had some effect. The sharks veered away, all but the largest one. The monster merely seemed pleased to ditch the competition.

Brianna released her grip on the child's hand. Tried to shake free so Ebby could escape. But the merchild didn't let go. Instead, Ebby gave Brianna a headshake to negate the idea. Did the little one have a plan?

The shark's mouth formed an oval of deadly teeth. Brianna pointed the net at it, hoping to at least force it to keep its distance. The shark was more agile and intelligent than she imagined, nosing the net aside so it could slide along the pole. At the last moment, Ebby jerked Brianna away. The beast's sandpapery side grazed Brianna's foot, leaving a burning welt in its wake.

Ebby turned, little tail churning water, and emitted another blast of song. The shark ignored it and circled back. The merchild's hold on Brianna tightened, shaking wildly. Brianna realized the child was no match for this beast, no matter how brave.

Gathering her strength, she jerked her hand free of the merchild's. She grasped her net with both hands and swung it down between her and the shark in a maddeningly slow arc. If she could lodge it in the creature's mouth, at least Ebby might be able to get away.

Ebby cried out again, and the shark twitched to the right.

Directly into the loop of the net.

The creature bolted forward, face in the net, and the hoop caught against its dorsal fin. Brianna's head rocked back at the sudden speed, her grip on the pole slipping slightly. The net seemed to both anger and confuse the beast. It twisted and rolled, trying to free itself. Brianna hung on like she held a tiger by the tail.

Ebby darted in front of the shark's nose, luring it along. The creature pulled determinedly, slowed by Brianna's weight. At first Brianna thought the merchild meant to use the shark to head home. Instead, Ebby turned into the current.

Back toward Zantu and the mermaids.

It appeared they really were going to take the tiger by the tail.

CHAPTER 11

ZANTU CLOSED HIS eyes and tried to ward off the effects of Loia's song. Her hands caressed his chest and arms, her endless song complimenting his physique, promising pleasures untold. One hand found his sheath, attempting to lure his cock free.

Then a second voice joined hers, battling for supremacy. He opened his eyes a slit. The raven-haired mermaid undulated in the filtered light, her iridescent skin shifting with mesmerizing color. Her crimson nipples pointed as sharply as the dart she'd hit him with. Her genital slit gaped suggestively, and he felt his cock respond with a will of its own.

Loia screeched in complaint, sending her veil of fish at the newcomer.

The dark one screeched back, "It was my dart that felled him!"

The water churned with foam and bits of slaughtered fish as the two engaged in a physical competition. The iridescent one spun and smacked Loia in the face with her scarred tail fin, drawing blood. Loia's hand flew to her mouth, and she reeled backward, her fish-harp sinking from sight.

The dark one rippled toward Zantu, a predatory grin on her lips.

Loia recovered and shot forward, mouth open to bury her pointed teeth in the other's shoulder.

And then a flash of gold as Didra slipped past the fight to press her coral-brown nipples against Zantu's chest. Her song in his ear was subtle, quiet, and deliciously inviting.

His cock surged against her genital slit. The helplessness from the love toxin clawed at his soul. Burned through his blood. Raged against the injustice of one sex that held so much power over the other. His fingernails bit into his palm as he commanded every muscle to fight the promise of pleasure.

Another angry screech, and Didra was ripped from him. Flashes of indigo, gold, and iridescent-black fins created an intoxicating dance. The water grew cloudy with fish parts and blood. Furious mer-song escalated as each mermaid attempted to outdo the other, their notes coalescing into a single, primal melody of lust.

His racing heart pulsed in his head, the tempo overriding the music in the churning water. He clenched his fists, focusing on the sensation of his fingernails biting into his palm. Perhaps the toxin was wearing off. If only he could slip away now, while they were busy competing with each other.

Out of nowhere, something slammed into the midst of the brawl. He barely had time to register the predatory shape of a massive shark—with a human trailing it like a lamprey...

Brianna? he sent.

There was too much chaos for him to sense anything in return. The cloudy water reddened with more than fish blood, and the mermaid's screams no longer carried a hint of seduction. *Brianna!* he sent. Surely he'd been imagining things? How could she be controlling a shark? Under the best circumstances, even mer-song couldn't exert much control over the beasts other than inciting them against each other. Brianna couldn't even sing.

He twitched his tail, pulling forth every bit of strength he had to fight off the waning toxin and regain mobility.

A voice reached him. Not through the water, but in his mind. *Zantu!*

Brianna? Where are you? I told you to run!

Out of the gory cloud emerged a small merchild followed by a clumsy, flailing human. The ravenous crunch of bones from within confirmed the shark was otherwise occupied.

Brianna's thought echoed with feverish energy. *We're here to save you.*

"Where's my dad?" Ebby cried.

Zantu was gaining strength by the moment and turned to point in the direction he remembered leaving Rubac. Ebby took his hand and began hauling both him and Brianna that way. As the toxin left his system, he joined the child's efforts.

He sent out a query and was answered by a weak version of Rubac's familiar song. Ebby released them and darted forward. Zantu took the moment to draw Brianna against his side. *You should not have come back.*

She wrapped her legs around him and buried her face against his neck. *I thought I'd lost you.*

How the depths did you wrangle a shark?

All I did was hang on. Ebby's quite the little scrapper. Her trembling body told him a bigger story.

He embraced her, savoring the scent of her hair and skin. His imagination churned with other more likely outcomes. *You got lucky this time.*

Rubac appeared through the hazy water, tail movements still uncoordinated from the effects of the toxin. Ebby held his hand, leading the way.

Zantu looked over Brianna's head to greet his brother. "What were you thinking, Rubac? The deeps are no place for a youngling."

"You refused to help." Rubac hung his head. "And Father used to bring us out here. Ebby wanted to come."

"I wanted to see a whale." Ebby looked into Rubac's face with a youth's oblivion to mortality. "But we lost the baby."

A part of Zantu felt sorry for his brother. "What happened?"

Rubac covered his face with both hands. Ebby wriggled up to give him a hug. The child answered for him. "Didra dropped it into the deeps."

The pity in Zantu's soul intensified, but there was nothing to be done. "The child is at one with the sea again. That's all anyone can ask for."

Gripping Brianna tight against him, he led the way back to the kelp forest.

ZANTU CARRIED a sleeping Brianna back to his nest and laid her on the sponge bed. He spent the night holding her, stroking her, making love with her, etching each moment into his memory so it would last a lifetime. He wanted her at his side forever, but if today's incident had taught him anything, it was that Brianna didn't belong in the ocean. She couldn't sing. She couldn't even hear the full range of notes the ocean carried. And even if the breath-bond could be made permanent, she couldn't defend herself; the net had been a lucky moment, one not likely to be repeated.

She belonged on land.

If she stayed with him in the ocean, it only meant death for them both. And while he'd die for her in a heartbeat, the thought of her dying because of his selfish need to keep her close was unacceptable. The only place she'd be safe was back among her kind.

He knew she would fight his decision. Resist his plan to send her back. How odd that he was about to execute the very thing he'd feared from the outset of his mate-bond.

At the first notes of the morning chorus, he lifted her gently and carried her out of the nest. Each coral-covered stone they passed on the way toward the shore felt like an added weight to Zantu's soul. He broke the surface as golden fingers of light glinted across the wavelets of the cove he'd chosen for her. His lungs felt tight with more than unaccustomed air as grief threatened to turn him back. He forced himself onward, knowing this was the only way to keep his mate safe. The pebbled beach was vacant in the morning light, but a small boat rested on the shore, and a house stood in sight of the water among wind-twisted trees on a rocky hill.

She roused as his tail scraped the rocky bottom, her sleepy thoughts reaching for him, seeking comfort.

Zantu? Where are we?

He set her feet against the floor. *You must go home, my angelfish.*

She groped for him, fingers slipping against his shoulders. *Wait! I don't understand!*

He gritted his teeth and dove beneath the waves, swimming fast and far out to sea.

Don't leave me! Zantu!

Her cries followed him clear to the edge of the wild deeps.

❧❧❧

ZANTU CRUISED the watery interface where the cold northern waters met the current off the kelp beds. Since abandoning Brianna, the dark waters of the wild deeps seemed to call his soul. He'd spent the last four moons scouring the bottom for treasure. His nest was crowded with human items, from gilded picture frames to unidentifiable plastic machines.

But none of it was the human thing he wanted.

He circled the long metal box from a cargo ship that had lodged on a ledge. This one appeared undamaged. The lower current's cold water had seeped into his bones, and his fingers were stiff as he lifted a chunk of basalt to bash the lock. Merpeople didn't have the layer of blubber that kept whales and other sea mammals warm in northern waters, and he'd already been down here past his usual endurance. But finding human artifacts was the only thing that interested him since leaving Brianna, so he kept at it.

The rusty metal lock crumbled under the impact. Once it was removed, he put a shoulder beneath the bar securing the door and pushed. The latch gave with a rusty, hollow grating sound, as did the hinges as he opened the door. He squinted and sent forth a sonic query to judge the contents.

Mounds of rotted textiles.

Disappointment sank him to the stony outcropping. Ruined by the sea. That seemed to be the story of most things human down here. Broken. Decayed. Unable to survive.

The familiar drumbeat of a whale reached him, and he realized he'd been resting too long. His joints were stiff with cold, and his heart seemed to struggle to beat. Going to sleep seemed like a good idea.

The whale thumped the water, calling to the krill it sought to consume. Whales were one of the few creatures, fish or mammal, to have words in its song. Rubac swore they were the keepers of myth and still grieved over the lost opportunity to elevate his child.

Zantu thought about his last meeting with one, when Brianna had been by his side. The creature hadn't denied the magic of elevation, so maybe the myth had some truth.

But it had said something else, too. Something just now returning to his memory. *I've not seen a mated human in over a century. You have much to learn.*

Zantu frowned, blood pumping a little harder. What was there to learn? Was there something he'd missed? Gathering his strength, he forced his cold muscles to carry him upward toward the whale's song.

He found the whale circling near the surface, its massive, scarred body black against the light.

"Great whale," Zantu called. The frigid waters had sapped him of his voice, and the whale took no notice of the small visitor, continuing its wide-mouthed sweep through the clouds of krill. He tried again. "Great whale, I have a question."

The whale continued to ignore him, thumping the water.

Zantu bolstered his song. "Please, I have a human bond-mate. I need your help."

The whale's thumping paused, its barnacled body slowing its loop through the swarm. It turned its great black eye upon him. "Bond-mate?" the creature grated. "How did this happen?"

The story flowed out like a riptide, of how he'd happened upon her, how she'd proven herself loyal, how he'd been forced to set her free. The retelling left Zantu mentally exhausted.

The whale resumed its circle through the krill. "If she cannot be with you, why do you not join her?"

Zantu's mind spun. "Join her? How would I do that?"

"Humans and merfolk separated ways not so very long ago in the timeline of the world. You can breathe air, can you not?"

Although mermen avoided the surface, Zantu had indeed breathed air a handful of times and knew that to be true. "Yes, but breathing air is only one piece of things. She lives on land. With legs."

The whale's drumbeat call sounded like laughter. "Have the merfolk truly lost all knowledge of their magic? As you can give the gift of the ocean with water breathing to her, she can give the gift of land to you."

Zantu's mind reeled. "Do you mean legs?"

"True bond-mates compromise to be together. Sometimes one gives more, sometimes another. It is the way of things if they wish to be together."

"I could live on land," Zantu said, rolling the words around as if tasting the idea.

"Indeed," the whale sang and swiped its tail to pursue the retreating cloud of krill.

"Wait! How?"

But the whale didn't stop. Its words floated back in an echo of song. "If you're bonded, you already know."

Zantu wasn't sure what that meant. But he meant to find out. Reenergized with new hope, he aimed himself for the surface.

CHAPTER 12

SURROUNDED BY THE scent of rotting seaweed and salt, Brianna rose from the damp stone and snapped shut the picnic basket that'd held her lunch. Facing the sea, she brushed bits of sand from her cotton capri pants. As always, the slate-gray ocean whispered to her, waves kissing the shore with promises never kept. Sometimes the water cleared the beach, leaving pristine pebbles glinting in the sun. Sometimes it left lines of garbage. Today the beach was clear.

She called with her mind as she did every time before she left the cove, *Zantu!*

As usual, only silence in return.

Perhaps her therapist was correct. Her time in the ocean had been a hallucination. Her mate a myth.

As if in disagreement, the child within her rolled, a sensation like tiny bubbles. She placed her hand over her barely rounded belly. "Don't worry, little one. I know I'm not crazy."

Upon her forced return to land, she'd climbed the stairs to the small house. The driftwood-gray structure had obviously been vacant for a long time, but the door was unlocked, and inside she'd found some old clothes. After a short walk down the dirt lane, she'd reached the highway, flagged down a car, and made it back to town.

Within the week, Eric had signed her divorce paperwork without question. Soon after, she'd discovered she was pregnant. The idea of raising a child alone broke her heart, but she knew there'd never be another man in her life. Zantu was her mate and always would be.

She'd bought the small cliff house overlooking Zantu's beach and taken a position at the nearby marine research center. Granted, she was only a bookkeeper, but being near the fish and other creatures felt like home.

And, sometimes, she swore she could hear them singing.

Placing her sandaled feet carefully over the uneven beach stones, she headed toward the stairs up to the house. The tide was coming in, and although she sometimes dreamed of throwing herself back into the ocean's embrace, she knew better than to hope to be saved a second time. Plus she now had another life to consider.

The brisk breeze at her back seemed to call her name as she walked, stones crunching beneath her feet. *Brianna...*

She paused, cocking her head and closing her eyes to accept the wind's caress. She often dreamed like this, her name upon her lover's lips, the sensation of the word along her skin.

Brianna...

She opened her eyes. This wasn't the wind. *Zantu?*

The baby rolled again, fluttering within her as if dancing to a song.

Brianna, I need you.

She spun to face the sea, nearly turning an ankle on the uneven stones. A silver tail splashed the water near the cliff.

"Zantu," she whispered, the air in her lungs refusing to move. Then, full force, she screamed, "Zantu!"

Heedless of her shoes, her clothes, her footing, she flung the picnic basket aside and ran into the waves. "Zantu, I'm here!"

A head appeared above the surface a little closer than before, silver hair blending with the gray-clouded horizon, then was gone.

She stopped as the water reached her waist, sandals slipping over the lumpy bottom. Waves lifted and dropped her. Had she imagined him? She watched the water, every ounce of her being calling to him. *I'm here!*

A length of silver materialized beneath the mirrored water in front of her, and then Zantu's naked gleaming torso rose.

"Oh my God." She stepped forward, slipped, fell into his arms. She threw kisses across his face, gulped water as they both went under, found his mouth to kiss.

He pushed her away, upward to the surface. *No.*

Gasping and choking, she clawed her hands against his shoulders, feet scrabbling to find the bottom. *Why are you here then? Please don't leave me again.*

He rose to face her, helping her stand. She gripped him tightly around the neck. Wrapped her legs around his hips. *I won't let you go. You have to take me with you.*

Chuckling against her hair, he shifted his hands down around to support her bottom and began moving to shore. He stumbled once but caught himself. He was *walking* to shore.

Brianna nearly let go. *"What..."*

I'm here for you, angelfish. It's your time to share magic with me.

Rising out of the water like an ancient god, he carried her toward the cliff.

"You're human!" She found herself speaking the words as she thought them. Still in shock, she lowered her feet to the ground to make him stop. *"Are you really here to stay?"*

"Yes." He used his real voice this time instead of only his mind. The word, although accented, was clear and deep and sexy as hell.

She stepped back, her gaze roving over his broad shoulders to his well-muscled stomach and lower, to where his member stood at half-mast amid sparse silver curls.

Where his tail had been he now had perfect, athletic legs. Her attention returned to his cock. "You're naked! And you're a man."

His cock twitched in response, rising to attention. "Yes, I am."

Tempting as he was, she forced her gaze back to his eyes. They were as silver as she remembered, his lips just as luscious. She raised one hand to trace a finger over the soft skin.

From down the beach, a child's voice snapped Brianna out of her lust. While her little cove was generally secluded, it was by no means private. There'd be time to explore Zantu later. Lots of time.

"You're going to need some clothes." She shrugged out of her windbreaker and wrapped it around his hips. It didn't cover everything, to her chagrin and delight, so she had to skew it sideways to hide the most important parts.

"Why do you get to undress and I have to dress?" He tugged at the knotted fabric, and she slapped his hand gently.

"You've got a lot to learn about humans."

"I'm looking forward to it."

She took his hand and led him past the curious stares of two children toting kites along the windswept beach. *Well, you're going to get to learn from the ground up —Daddy.*

His moment of confusion was followed by a joyful shout that echoed from the rocky cliffs and drew giggles from the nearby children. He swept her into his arms and spun her as she giggled.

Together they climbed the stairs to their nest overlooking the ocean. She'd found her mate. Her true love. The father of her children.

Dearest Reader,

Thank you for reading The Merman's Kiss! I hope you enjoyed your underwater escape with Zantu and Briana. The next book in the Mates for Monsters series is THE MERMAN'S QUEST. Find out what happens to Zantu's brother, Rubac, now that he no longer has a mate...

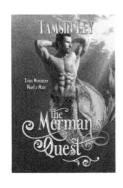

Tap the cover to get your copy now or keep reading for an excerpt!

P.S. Your help spreading the word, including telling a friend or leaving a review on your favorite books site, means the world to me. Reviews help readers find books! If you want to stay in touch, sign up for my VIP newsletter. Members get exclusive giveaways, sneak peeks of future books, and bonus scenes. There's an exclusive deleted scene from The Merman's Kiss waiting for you right now!

SIGN UP FOR TAMSIN'S NEWSLETTER:
https://bookhip.com/RHMKCM

Turn the page for a short excerpt from The Merman's Quest...

The boat's engine sputtered to life, backfired, and died. With a curse, Madison shut everything down and moved to the engine compartment to adjust the choke. *Stupid rental.* She was going to be pissed if she had to call for a tow back to land.

A high, sweet note bounced across the water like a small child's laugh. *What was that?* She raised her head and searched the waves. The note shifted into something like a sultry oboe or saxophone holding a long note accompanied by a compulsive rhythm like a heartbeat. Was there another vessel nearby playing music? She couldn't see one.

She closed her eyes, taking a breath of sweet, salty air before opening them again to search for the song's source. The sun glittered like diamonds across the water's surface, forcing her to squint. Was that a man swimming toward her?

He disappeared below the surface, and the song thrummed through the deck against her feet. The pulse crept up her legs in delightful shivers to concentrate in her core. *God, that feels good.* Next thing she knew, she was standing at the gunwale.

A dark haired man surfaced about six meters away, closely-trimmed beard dripping water. He had the broad shoulders and lean, muscular torso of a speed swimmer. A spiral shell earring curled through one earlobe, and a large sliver of mother-of-pearl pierced his nipple in one well-sculpted left pec. He stroked a mesmerizing rhythm over a white pronged object hanging from a cord about his neck, seemingly unperturbed about being adrift at sea. What struck her most, however, was the lime-green shade of his eyes. A sense of vertigo blossomed in her stomach, and she yearned to escape the rocking motion of the deck. She leaned against the gunwale to steady herself.

"Hello? Do you need help?" She didn't know what else to ask. He was too far out to have come from shore.

He opened his mouth, and the shockingly physical melody that had driven her to the side swelled louder.

Her core tightened with surprising intensity, deliciously orgasmic. The scientist in her distantly wondered if orgasm by auditory stimulation was even possible. Then stopped analyzing and allowed the sensation to sweep her along as if it were a curling green wave. Her nipples pebbled against her shirt and warmth pooled deep in her belly. She gripped both hands on the lip of the gunwale, legs trembling.

The man dove, revealing what looked like a lacy green dorsal fin along his spine. A bright green tail followed, the billowing fin sending a shower of water her direction. She blinked, regaining a fleeting moment of scientific curiosity. *Had that been...? No way.* Then the song changed back into that bone-deep rhythm, rising through the deck, through her legs. Pounding against her pelvis as if a man thrust deep inside her.

Inhaling sharply, she threw back her head, lost in the ecstasy. The tide of primal sensation overwhelmed her logic. Every inch of her skin thrilled with electric desire, and she ached to be touched. Now.

Her hand crept to her breast, fondled her nipple to an aching peak. She needed more. She needed this man, who was somehow calling up her basest emotions. Leaning over, one hand on the gunwale while the other still pinched her nipple, she peered into the water. Where'd he gone?

His face appeared directly below, rising to meet her. A pair of lime-green eyes bored into hers with a come-hither purpose to match the vibrations in her bones. She stretched forward, heeding the call.

He broke the surface and met her lips with his. The contact sent her spiraling into climax. Her grip on the gunwale fell slack and she plunged past him into the icy water...

Get your copy of The Merman's Quest and keep reading!

ACKNOWLEDGMENTS

You, my critique partners, know who you are. I thank you for letting me pick your brains, for your generous time, and for your continued input when I set a date with my editor that our critique schedule cannot possibly meet. This story wouldn't be here without you.

Galactic Pirate Brides series

Galactic Pirate Brides Box Set (Includes first 3 books)

Rescued by Qaiyaan

Ransomed by Kashatok

Claimed by Noatak

Mates for Monsters

Mer-Lovers Collector's Edition (Includes first 3 books)

The Merman's Kiss

The Merman's Quest

A Mermaid's Heart

The Centaur's Bride

The Djinn's Desire

Khargals of Duras

Sticks and Stones

Alaska Alphas

Alpha Origins

Untamed Instinct

Bewitched Shifter

Midnight Heat

POST-APOCALYPTIC SCIENCE FICTION WRITTEN AS TAM LINSEY

Botanicaust

The Reaping Room

Doomseeds

Amarantox

ABOUT THE AUTHOR

Once upon a time I thought I wanted to be a biomedical engineer, but experimenting on lab rats doesn't always lead to happy endings. Now I blend my nerdy infatuation of science with character-driven romance and guaranteed happily-ever-afters. My monsters always find their mates, with feisty heroines, tortured heroes, and all the steamy trouble they can handle. I promise my stories will never leave you hanging (although you may still crave more!)

When I'm not writing, I'll be in the garden or the kitchen, exploring Alaska with my husband, or preparing for the zombie apocalypse. I also love wine and hard apple cider, am mediocre at crochet, and have the cutest 12-pound bunny named Abigail.

Interested in more about me? Join my VIP Club and get free books, notices, and other cool stuff!

www.tamsinley.com

bookbub.com/authors/tamsin-ley

goodreads.com/TamsinLey

facebook.com/TamsinLey

amazon.com/author/tamsin

Made in the USA
Las Vegas, NV
31 May 2021

23978856R00089